D1291466

Pel and the Precious Parcel

PEL AND THE PRECIOUS PARCEL

Juliet Hebden

Constable · London

First published in Great Britain 1997
by Constable & Company Ltd
3 The Lanchesters, 162 Fulham Palace Road
London W6 9ER
Copyright © 1997 by Juliet Hebden
The right of Juliet Hebden to be identified
as the author of this work has been asserted
by her in accordance with the Copyright,
Designs and Patents Act 1988
ISBN 0 09 478160 5
Set in Palatino 10pt by
SetSystems Ltd, Saffron Walden
Printed and bound in Great Britain by
MPG Books Ltd, Bodmin, Cornwall

A CIP catalogue record for this book
is available from the British Library

For
John and Harriette
who help

1

It was a sad moment when Yves Pasquier asked Chief Inspector Pel to assist at the burial of their mutual friend. They stood together and stared silently down into the grave. A group of swallows were swooping high overhead, black silhouettes in an achingly blue sky, and on the heat haze the brightly coloured butterflies played hide and seek between the flowers. It was a beautiful day that made death incongruous and ugly.

'Nothing could have been done for him,' Yves said resolutely.

'He had a happy life,' Pel added.

'I suppose so, but I'll miss him.'

Pel lit a cigarette and inhaled deeply. 'I never could tell which end bit until he started wagging his tail.' He offered the packet of Gauloises to Yves. 'Still, fourteen was a good age for a dog.'

Yves puffed silently on his cigarette for a moment then, seizing the shovel, he began piling earth on to the animal's inert body.

'I see you smoke like a professional,' Pel observed.

'Since my eighteenth birthday I've gone public, my parents can't say a thing any more.'

Pel stared at the boy wide-eyed. It was only yesterday the child was galloping about brandishing a plastic Star Wars gun and chasing imaginary aliens behind the bushes. How dare he grow up without his permission? Looking at him now Pel was surprised to find that Yves was a good deal taller than he remembered, must have had what they called a growth spurt, if that was the expression, it sounded jolly rude to him. Nevertheless, he went on up a long time after Pel stopped. The detective shuffled inside his clothes and sighed: most people did. And Yves had long wavy blond hair; Pel had thinning grey hair that was giving up the struggle for survival. And he didn't wear glasses; Pel was half blind without his, screwing up his eyes to search into a blurred infinity. And he was damned intelligent, a baccalaureat with honours, off to university to study medicine at the end of the summer.

'Are you allowed to drink pastis?' he asked, watching the strapping young man gently pat the grave flat and erect a small home-made cross.

Yves gave his eyes a rub. 'Sure, it's just what I need right now,' he said shakily. 'No girl ever made me cry, but the bloody dog's managing it. I haven't blubbed like this in years, what the hell's the matter with me?'

'You've grown up,' Pel told him.

Yves wasn't entirely sure that he understood but he smiled and nodded, then followed his neighbour back through the hedge and into his kitchen for a drink.

'So I suppose fishing's off the agenda?' Pel asked him, handing over the cigarettes again.

'Oh, I don't know. No one's ever too grown up to go fishing.'

It was something, Pel thought. The little boy next door had reached adulthood, an adult who smoked, drank and went out with girls, but at least they could still go fishing together – when Yves was free from his studies and he was free from police work. Perhaps one day before both of them joined the bloody dog in heaven. And that was another thing; if heaven existed would St Pierre let a cantankerous old bugger like him through the pearly gates, and if he did what the hell would he do there with all those angelic souls? Be bored to tears probably. What a life! All those years of slogging his guts out to catch a few thousand criminals just so he could be bored rigid in heaven. If St Pierre let him in. And if he didn't . . .?

Fortunately for Pel the telephone cut abruptly into his thoughts. He picked up the receiver and looked at it as if it would bite him.

'*J'écoute*,' he shouted.

'They just held up a plane at the airport,' Darcy told him.

'Who?'

'Who knows? However, your presence would be appreciated. I'm going there now, I'll pick you up in a couple of minutes.'

'Holy Mother of God!' Pel cried. 'I can't even bury an old friend without interruptions.'

'Sorry, Patron, but the place is in a panic. Thought you'd like to be in on it.'

And of course his second-in-command was absolutely right. Pel would have hanged, drawn and quartered him if he hadn't been informed immediately.

'Help yourself to another one,' Pel said to Yves, pointing at the bottle, 'but no more than one. You might have grown up and gone public but I still have to live next door to your parents.'

The airport was surprisingly calm. Holiday-makers were coming and going through the automatic doors dragging cases after them; pretentious young businessmen with shining attaché cases marched back and forth talking importantly into mobile telephones. Pel suspected that most of them were ringing their wives or girlfriends for a chat simply to show off their newly acquired toy. It seemed to be an illness that was highly contagious; small black boxes with thick aerials sprouted from almost every breast pocket to be grabbed and attached to ears with an aggressive sweep of the hand. It was the modern salute to impress all passing strangers. Pel was not impressed, he was practising a well-worn scowl on whoever dared to notice. In the car he'd been boiled alive by an unrelenting sun streaming through the windscreen, his handkerchief doing little to alleviate the inevitable outbreak of perspiration. Now he risked frost-bite; the air-conditioning in the airport was working at full blast and making him shiver.

'Move along, please don't loiter.' An officious security man tried pushing Pel and Darcy out of the way but Pel wouldn't budge.

'Sir, I'm asking you to get out of the way. I'm expecting a very important policeman to arrive any moment.'

'Chief Inspector Pel, of the Police Judiciaire de la République de France, by any chance?' Darcy asked casually.

The security man stopped pushing and looked suspiciously at him. 'Yes, as a matter of fact,' he said slowly. 'How did you know?'

Darcy flipped open his wallet to reveal the identity card with the unmistakable red, white and blue stripe across it that shouted *flic* at everyone. 'Let me introduce you,' he said, turning towards Pel.

After profuse apologies they were finally taken behind the scenes to the man in charge of the airport. His office was already full of officials all yapping excitedly at one another, except for one, the man in charge. Monsieur Aubert, a large man with very little hair, was sitting at his desk cradling his head in his hands; he looked as if he was suffering from a migraine.

'Where are the passengers?' Pel asked Darcy quietly.

'Down in the VIP lounge with Nosjean, de Troq', Angelface and Annie.'

'Good God! You've emptied the Hôtel de Police.'

'There are rather a lot of passengers, Patron.'

The long-suffering Monsieur Aubert appeared to regain

consciousness as the two policemen approached and he manoeuvred his ample body wearily round the desk towards them.

'Who are you and what do you want?' he asked, trying unsuccessfully to refasten his tie. When he saw their identification his round face broke into a relieved smile.

'At last,' he said, shaking their hands vigorously, 'Chief Inspector Pel, now perhaps we'll make some sense of all this. Let's get out of here and go down to see the crew, they at least won't be hysterical.'

The crew were sitting calmly drinking coffee in a small and very private sitting-room not far from Aubert's animated office. They consisted of the pilot, the co-pilot, a male steward and two beautiful hostesses. It looked more like an intimate coffee party than the aftermath of a robbery; judging by the laughter they'd been enjoying themselves.

'It was the prettiest hold-up I've ever seen,' the pilot told them gaily. 'The flight from Montpellier had been a doddle with blue skies all the way. We got the all-clear from the control tower and came down on to the runway, putting on the brakes after we touched down. We came to a halt on the other side of the field and were preparing for the cruise back to the buildings and disembarkation when two cars pulled up in front of us. Between them was a large white sheet with "Shut off the engines or we open fire" clearly marked in black. A couple of men, armed to the teeth, jumped out and started waving their guns at us, so I thought the best thing to do was to comply. Once it had gone quiet I was told to open the forward baggage compartment. Well, I can't from the cockpit, which is what I told them. One of the men fired a couple of shots into the air, so I decided it was time to make my announcement to the passengers and get the kids on board into the middle of the bus. While I was doing this two more blokes hopped out of the cars and

11

ran to the plane. I thought for a moment we were going to have a fight on our hands but all they did was force the forward hold open. They got what they wanted, leapt back into the cars and scarpered to the fence. As soon as they'd turned their backs on us, I radioed for help and the airport police arrived as the men rode off into the sunset. It was brilliant, much neater than any stage-coach hold-up I've ever seen on the telly.'

Pel didn't share his opinion. 'What did these men look like?' he asked coldly.

'God knows.' The pilot grinned magnanimously. 'They were wearing mechanics' overalls, zipped to the top, rubber boots and stormtrooper hoods with just slits for their eyes and mouth.' He paused to think. 'Oh, and black gloves,' he added triumphantly.

It was no better than Pel had expected. 'Do you know what they got away with?'

'It looked like bags of potatoes,' the pilot announced calmly, 'but I doubt they'd have gone to all that trouble for a few kilos of spuds. On the cargo manifest it was described as "perfumery samples" belonging to Blau Beauté of Sète.' He showed Pel his pilot's log of cargo loaded at Montpellier. 'The bandits knew what they were after,' he added. 'They broke in, took the bags and made off with them – they didn't touch the other hold.'

'These bags,' Pel asked, 'they were just loose in the hold?'

'Nope, they'd been delivered in a wired crate. It was loaded at the same time as the five containers from La Poste, but they didn't touch those.'

'So they forced open the hold, cut the wires then prised the lid off the crate?'

The pilot nodded and took a sip at his coffee. '*C'est exacte*,' he said.

Pel frowned. 'Who else had a copy of this manifest?'

'Oh, dozens of people,' the pilot replied gaily. 'Half a

dozen copies would have been floating about in Montpellier, another half-dozen here, plus the fact that it would have been on the computers.'

'Darcy, get on to Montpellier and the man responsible for unloading here . . .' but Darcy was already on his way.

The small jet that had been robbed had arrived on time and, after its short delay at the end of the runway, its fifty-two passengers, impatiently answering the policemen's questions, were anxious to get on with their lives and out of the airport.

'No one was hurt,' a smart young man announced, clutching his bleeping telephone to his ear. 'I can't see what the fuss is about. Hold the line, please,' he said to the little black box. 'Look, I've an important meeting in the city, I've made a statement, I'd like to leave.'

Pel looked at Aimedieu's angelic face. He'd been busy scribbling but he stopped to shrug his shoulders. 'I've no more questions, Patron.'

'Then you may go,' Pel agreed. 'Aimedieu, see him through security at the door.' He watched the man go, his telephone still pressed importantly to the side of his head. Pel was convinced the meeting in the city was no more than lunch with a delicious little blonde.

He went from group to group and when he was satisfied that all names and addresses, plus a short statement from each witness, were being efficiently taken, he left them to it and marched off to find the head of the airport police, Monsieur Moreau.

'Less than three minutes,' the burly man in uniform wailed, staring out at the tarmac through his office window. 'The plane came to a stop, they helped themselves and were gone in a cloud of dust before we knew anything about it.'

'The pilot radioed through for help as soon as the danger was over,' Pel pointed out.

'Indeed, but they were right at the end of the runway.

13

They had only a few metres to cover to the perimeter fence, we had miles.' He looked as if he were about to burst into tears as he turned to offer Pel a cigarette from a well-crumpled packet.

The two of them sat and smoked, turning over the events between them. It had been a highly professional and cheeky job. The two cars might give them some clues, when they were found; an *avis de recherche* had gone out immediately for two dark-coloured family saloons each carrying two men but so far there was no news. It was hardly surprising. Forensics had turned up and were going over the small jet with a fine-tooth comb. It was going to take time.

Blau Beauté had been informed and their legal representative, Maître Theron, after a slight hesitation, was now screaming at the airline threatening to sue them for insufficient security, screaming at the airport authorities for being slipshod and slow, screaming at the pilots' union because there had been no resistance from the cockpit, in fact screaming at anyone and everyone he could find. He shouted that a handsome reward was being considered for any information leading to the recovery of the perfumery samples, which were very valuable, but Pel and Moreau knew they weren't eligible even if they recovered the lot. It was a hard life being a policeman.

'An inside job?' Pel suggested, settling himself into his own comfortable office and reaching for one of the open packets of Gauloises nestling between the piles of paperwork.

'Who knows?' Darcy replied, deftly scooping up a stray cigarette and lighting it before his boss had time to stop him.

'Darcy, will you stop saying, "Who knows?" and get

yourself in gear. Did you get the list of airport personnel?'
Pel snapped, trying to light his own cigarette with a series
of matches. He broke two, discarded three duds and
finally managed to burn his finger ends.

Darcy clicked his electronic *briquet* into action and Pel
was lost behind a cloud of thick blue smoke.

'I also have a list of people working for Blau Beauté,
Patron,' he said as the fog cleared. 'It's a family firm with
only twenty-one employees. That and the list from the
airport – all sixty-six pages of it, including even the taxi
drivers with permits to work there and the car-park
attendants, sorry, they prefer to be called technicians – are
with Debray. He's fastidiously punching the names into
his computer to see if he can come up with likely suspects.
As soon as he's completed the operation he has instructions to report directly to you in the event that there's a
possible, and to me if there's nothing. He's also making a
search on another computer for similar crimes in Europe
and collating the whereabouts of the perpetrators. In the
meantime, one team from Forensics are still crawling all
over the hold of the aircraft collecting and labelling every
bit of fluff they find, but only after Fingerprints and
Photography have finished their job, sir!'

Pel sighed. 'There's no need to be facetious.'

'Sorry, Patron.' Darcy smiled and inhaled with satisfac-
tion on his stolen cigarette. Pel decided he should be fired.

'It was quite a daring little caper,' Darcy went on. 'They
must have spent a long time working out the logistics.
Someone with above average criminal intelligence must
be behind it. Holding up an aircraft,' he said, 'it's the sort
of thing you'd expect from – '

Pel interrupted him. 'It's no good jumping to conclusions and it's not the sort of thing I expect from anyone
– now get out and let me think.'

But thinking wasn't what the day had lined up for Pel.
The telephone buzzed and he forced himself to answer.

'Sorry to bother you, Chief Inspector, I know you must be frantically busy,' the head of airport security said. Pel was beginning to like the man, he understood the hardships of his life. 'My chaps have just made their verbal report to me and I thought you'd like to know how they got in.'

'I don't give a damn about how your chaps got in,' Pel replied absently, reading a fax from Montpellier he hadn't noticed before.

'No, sir,' Moreau said patiently. 'I mean how the bandits got into the grounds of the airport.'

Pel screwed up the fax viciously and threw it at the wastepaper basket; as usual, he missed.

'Go on then,' he said, '*accouche*.'

'It was through a service entrance at that side of the airfield. They simply cut through the heavy-duty padlock, opened the gates and drove into position as the plane was touching down.'

'No one noticed them?'

'We're a small airport, everyone was busy watching the landing, not the perimeter fence, it's not yet on the central surveillance computer system. It's not unusual for sightseers to park in that spot to watch the planes come and go. I was listening to the control tower at the time. Once the plane was down, clearance was given to a private jet taking off for Paris, and the first we knew of the hold-up was when we heard the captain's announcement to his passengers to remain calm and to move the children aboard into the middle of the plane. He must have left the channel open deliberately, knowing the announcement would put us on alert. It's standard procedure if there are bullets flying about outside, although, I must confess, it's the first time we've heard it here.'

'What about the gunshots?'

'They were obliterated by the noise of the Paris flight revving up and taking off. It took them two and a half minutes to do the job. Our men were ready to move in forty-five seconds after I heard the alert but we couldn't close in until the captain had said it was safe to do so or we could have endangered lives.' He sighed deeply. 'We arrived half a minute after they'd left.'

'Why didn't you give chase?'

'The two cars went in opposite directions and we were more concerned with getting the passengers safely off in case they'd planted a bomb in the hold. It happens, you know.'

Pel pushed his glasses up on to his head. The information didn't help at all, but he thanked Moreau and replaced the receiver only to snatch it up again before he'd had a chance to finish inhaling forcefully on a newly lit cigarette. His words caught in his throat and caused a coughing fit violent enough to turn his face purple. He gasped out his words as if they were his last.

'I've always told you cigarettes are dangerous,' the caller told him. 'Your asthma sounds serious.'

'Never mind my asthma,' Pel growled. 'What do you want, Leguyder?'

Leguyder was head of Forensics and, while he was extremely efficient at his job, he was anti-smoking and a bore. Pel suspected he read the *Encyclopaedia Larousse* in the evening so he could blind them all with useless information the following day. However, Pel needed his expertise and forced himself to be patient.

'I'm ringing to tell you that the lorryload of rubbish I've just received from the number one hold of Flight M502 is going to take a very long time to sift through. Don't they ever clean them out? For instance, I have in my possession no fewer than thirty-five chewing gum wrappers, three hundred and fifteen assorted pieces of fluff, enough twigs and leaves to – '

Pel didn't wait to find out. 'Get on with it – have you any clues?'

17

'I'm already dramatically overworked and my lab technicians – '

'Is that all?'

'What do you mean, is that all? You don't seem to realise how heavily everyone depends on the Forensic Science department. We don't just work for the police, you know. If it wasn't for us . . .'

Pel gently put the phone down and drew luxuriously on his nerve-calming Gauloise. If Leguyder had anything of interest he'd be back to gloat over his findings and impress them all with long words that no one understood.

'And what are you waiting for?' Pel shouted at Darcy who was still lingering by the door smiling at him.

'To find out what the fax was all about, and to know whether I should have leapt into action before it arrived.'

'Yes, you should. It was the bloody Blau family who lost their bags of potatoes to the bandits. They're sending a delegation to inform us of the consequences.'

Darcy raised his eyebrows. 'Potatoes?'

Sighing, Pel pushed his glasses up on to his forehead. 'You know what I mean,' he said. 'Apparently the stolen cargo was worth a hell of a lot of money – no doubt we'll find out exactly how much when they arrive.'

'Let's hope it's not the robbery of the century.' Darcy grinned, flashing his perfect white teeth.

Pel scowled. He had a feeling of impending doom.

2

The delegation from Montpellier arrived at the Hôtel de Police at 15.37 that afternoon. That was the time logged at the front desk by the efficient young sergeant on duty. It took them three and a half minutes to be escorted to Pel's office door and as long for them to shake hands and settle into the waiting chairs. The Chief was informed but told Darcy that he wasn't in and Pel would have to cope. He disliked delegations and was enjoying the thought of Pel's predicament. Although he respected Pel's ability as a policeman, he recognised that his chief inspector was a difficult little bugger and just occasionally it was a pleasure to get his own back for the headaches Pel caused.

At that moment Pel was scowling beautifully behind his glasses and rapidly lighting a Gauloise before passing the packet automatically to Darcy standing alongside. Confronted by delegations from anywhere, Pel considered any other policeman a partner in crime.

'*Je vous écoute*,' he said to the group seated in an uncomfortable line in front of him. Three men and one woman, all smart with carefully combed hair and shining shoes. Each one of them had an important-looking brief-case resting by their chair and the youngest of the four, the one who was speaking, had a suspicious-looking aerial poking out of his jacket pocket.

'I'm Maître Paul Pascal Theron and I am the legal representative for Blau Beauté,' he said. 'On my right is the managing director, Madame Maxine Blau-Rolland.' She bowed her attractive head almost invisibly. Pel didn't like the look of her either; her skin was too smooth and perfectly tanned, her eyes were too cold and blue, her

19

mouth was a blood-red slit and she wore huge ear-rings that looked like satellite dishes. Perhaps it was for better reception on her mobile telephone – he wondered where she'd hidden it.

'Beside Madame is the personal lawyer of Monsieur Josephe Blau, Maître Guy Delmas,' P.P. Theron continued. 'He has consented to represent the chairman of the company as it was felt it would be wiser for someone of Monsieur Blau's age not to travel.' Pel decided Delmas looked like a small pale Shylock. 'And on my left Monsieur Pierre Fabré, a specialist from the perfumery department of Blau Beauté.'

Pel stared at them, knowing full well he'd never remember their names or what they did; he hoped like hell that Darcy was concentrating hard. He gave him a quick glance and, seeing his colleague casually watching the smoke curling up from his cigarette, he relaxed. When Darcy looked as if he was dreaming his brain was on remote control – he'd remember the lot.

P.P. Theron droned on at length, describing how Madame Blau-Rolland's elderly father had parcelled up the samples personally and handed them over to a security firm who delivered them to Montpellier airport, stressing to everyone concerned that they were very valuable. Another security firm had been assigned to receive the crate at this end with instructions to take it to Crédit Agricole in the city.

'What exactly was in the crate?' Pel asked.

'Very precious perfume samples,' P.P. Theron replied dully. 'Monsieur Blau is the only one who knows exactly what it contained – quantities, volumes, et cetera.'

'Had contact been made with the bank here?'

'Of course,' Maître Delmas said. 'My client told me that arrangements here had been satisfactorily made.'

'With whom?'

'Monsieur Blau senior would not tell me.'

20

'I think it would be advantageous', Theron said, 'to let our specialist take over and explain what was probably in the consignment.' The expert opened his mouth but it was Madame Blau-Rolland who spoke.

'You must realise these samples were of the greatest importance and value,' she said. 'They were prototypes, so to speak, there are no duplicates. We are a small firm producing beauty products and for some time we have been trying to break into the perfume market. Our "noses", as they are called, have experimented with thousands of scents. The samples in that crate were the result of years of work. If one of our competitors gets their hands on them all our efforts will be rendered worthless.'

'Do you think it may have been industrial sabotage?' Pel asked, raising a weary eyebrow at the well-polished businesswoman.

'We believe this could be the case.'

'But it was your elderly father, madame, who was responsible for the shipping of the precious consignment.'

'My father is eighty-one years old.' She sighed heavily. 'He knows he hasn't got long to live but likes to feel he still runs the business. Yes, I let him make the necessary arrangements although,' she added, 'obviously I oversee his every move. I had of course been present on and off while he was preparing the crate.'

'So you were indirectly responsible for the transportation?'

'I suppose you could put it like that,' she agreed haughtily.

'It may be that I don't understand the workings of the perfume trade,' Pel said calmly, 'but could you tell me why these samples were destined for a bank?'

'For safety,' Madame snapped, as if Pel was an idiot.

'Why here?' he insisted. 'Why not Montpellier?'

'It was my father's wish. He's an old man losing the

grip he's had on the firm he created as a young man and he knows it. When the board decided we should branch out into perfume he opposed us. However, we went ahead, believing he could be persuaded. He was, and he became more and more interested in the secrecy surrounding our tests. When the samples were finished he wanted to take part in moving them from the factory to a safer place until we were ready for production. He insisted Montpellier would be the first place our competitors would look and told us it had to be here. Because it was so illogical we were convinced no one would think of it, therefore we decided to humour him and proceed.'

'But why this city?'

'Why not? It's not so dreadful here.'

'Madame!' Pel drew himself to his full height, which wasn't much, particularly as he was sitting down. 'You are talking about the capital of Burgundy, the most beautiful city in France, indeed in the world. A city of culture, of history, of – '

'So you're proud of your city,' she interrupted, 'but I haven't got a clue why the samples were to be stored here. It wouldn't surprise me if my father closed his eyes and stuck a pin in the map – he's capable of it.'

'You don't seem very fond of your father, madame,' Pel retorted more calmly.

Her eyes widened with indignation. 'I love my father, monsieur,' she replied, as if she was announcing the arrival of a train at platform five, 'but he is a very old and sometimes an irrational man. For a long time he gave up going into the office. It was only after we had almost reached the conclusion of our tests that he brightened up and started causing mayhem at the factory again. As a working woman, my time is money but I also take care of him – for instance, he lives with my husband and me – and that alone can be a full-time job. So you see, I am extremely fond of my father, though perhaps a little tired of his unnecessary interference. It's time he retired for good.'

It was a reasonable explanation and very well rehearsed. Pel decided he wasn't going to get much more useful information out of her but made a mental note to see the old man himself. He wondered if he'd stolen the samples from his own firm and intended doing a deal with a competitor as a final statement of his independence and power before his daughter boxed him up and sent him off to an old people's home for ever.

P.P. Theron then told him that the reward originally considered by Blau Beauté had been rejected. 'I acted in the interest of my clients,' he explained, 'but am told that it should never have been proposed unless it was my practice that was prepared to pay. It is not.'

'Therefore no reward,' Pel concluded. 'Were the samples insured?'

'The airline insures against damage to or loss of cargo in their possession.'

'But Blau Beauté?'

'My father didn't think of things like that,' Madame said crossly.

'And you, madame?'

'I have discussed the reward with my husband,' she replied, side-stepping away from the subject of insurance, 'who is also a director of the company, and we feel it would be wiser not to offer one. As he explained to me, he believes that the offer of a reward would draw the attention of our competitors and put at risk the final recovery of the samples. They are devious enough to put out their own higher reward to get their hands on the perfume and rob us of our eventual success in their market – if they haven't already done so, of course. I agree with his analysis of the situation and', she added, 'we have great confidence in the French police. We are sure that if recovery is possible you will succeed.'

23

Pel wondered how she could talk for so long and so forcefully without ever drawing breath. Perhaps she didn't smoke. He didn't trust people who didn't smoke. He'd have to check if she'd taken out a large insurance: it could be plain robbery, or industrial sabotage, or it could be a load of worthless bottles of scent which had been over-insured and deliberately removed so that Blau Beauté could make their claim and recuperate the cost of years of research ending with a perfume that smelt no better than a dog's bottom. The thought made him smile and he watched them leave to catch their private plane back to their private lives. By the look on Darcy's face he'd had the same idea.

'One asks oneself why they bothered,' Pel said.

'They bothered quite a bit,' Darcy pointed out.

'Precisely.'

'So I'd better get out of your office and on with the investigation, which is growing in enormity with every Gauloise we smoke.' Darcy grinned, reaching for Pel's packet of cigarettes.

Pel slammed his hand over them. 'Smoke your own,' he growled.

The two policemen left the office an hour later for a meeting with the director of Crédit Agricole but returned shortly afterwards with no further information. The director had been as helpful as possible but stated clearly that he had never heard of Blau Beauté before he was asked to receive a box of samples and to put them in his safe. Further instructions would have been forthcoming as soon as the crate arrived. He'd also told them that they were not accustomed to requests of this sort but wanted to be of assistance to a prospective client.

'At a price,' Darcy had suggested, and the director had

smiled his sly banker's smile. 'Naturally there would have been a charge made for such a service,' he'd agreed.

The security firm that had made the delivery in Montpellier and the firm that should have picked it up at the airport in Burgundy were contacted but had nothing to add; they had carried out their orders to the letter and it wasn't their fault. Pel insisted, however, on a complete list of their employees and after a short argument about the integrity of such firms was able to hand it over to Debray and his computer in the hope that they might be able to turn something up.

And two of his team were checking the insurance companies in Montpellier. There were twelve pages of them, with four columns covering each page, and the companies were hesitant about giving out information over the phone. By the end of the day voices were being raised in the sergeants' room: the opinion there was that insurance agents should be boiled in oil.

After his normal bad night's sleep, Pel arrived at the Hôtel de Police with his frown firmly in place. The duty sergeant wished him a good morning and as usual received no reply; he shrugged and went back to his paperwork, reassured that everything was normal.

The walking encyclopaedia, Leguyder, was sitting patiently in Pel's office holding a weighty report. He was looking forward to reading the entire document to the chief inspector and watching his eyes glaze over at all the long words, if only the little blighter would turn up.

Going at a reasonable speed down the corridor, Pel avoided a head-on collision with Nosjean, who'd accelerated unexpectedly through an open door. Finishing an inelegant hop, skip and jump, he looked at the young inspector. He reminded Pel of a youthful Napoleon on the bridge at Lodi, but this morning Napoleon's brow was furrowed.

'How's the baby?' Pel asked.

Nosjean sighed. 'Crying.'

'And your wife, Mijo?'

'Tired.'

'You don't look so hot yourself.'

'Being a married man with a six-month-old daughter is bad enough but I'm a married policeman – it doesn't help. By the way,' he went on, visibly brightening, 'Leguyder's waiting for you in your office with a report as thick as a telephone directory.'

'Then escort me to the morning meeting.'

The men were assembled in the sergeants' room checking their reports and calmly discussing the day ahead. Except for Misset who, with his brain in neutral, was slouched as usual in a corner, a cigarette hanging from his bottom lip, scratching his ever-increasing stomach while eyeing Annie Saxe's rump as she leaned over a map to point something out to Cheriff. Outside the door Pel stopped; he took a deep breath and exploded into the room. It was hardly worth it. Only Misset jumped to attention, dropping his sun-glasses on the floor with a clatter; the others barely moved.

'Well?' Pel shouted. 'Look lively, I've got work to do even if you lot haven't.' His team sorted themselves out and expected the worst.

Darcy went through the various cases they were working on, nothing more than a mere million muggings, drunk and disorderlies, frauds, swindles, a few thousand household fights, extortions, threats, bar brawls and grievous bodily harms. Nothing out of the ordinary for a day in the life of a member of the Police Judiciaire, until they came finally to the airport hold-up. Pujol, a relatively new boy, licked his lips and cautiously raised a hand.

26

'Yes,' Pel hissed.

Pujol cowered but persisted. 'I met Leguyder in the corridor,' he explained, 'and walked with him to your office where he's waiting to give you all the details on what they found in the hold of the plane, but basically there was nothing out of the ordinary, in other words, no clues. He also wanted to tell you that the lock and the wires round the box in the hold of the plane were cut open with the same cutters that destroyed the chain on the service gate to the airfield. The cutters were taken away with them, but by the look of the marks left, they weren't new, just an ordinary pair of *tenailles*, of which there must be millions. The guns were described as "like the rifles cowboys carry in Westerns".' Pel put his head in his hands. This hold-up was getting out of control, the citizens in the stage-coach had even seemed to enjoy watching the outlaws get away with the army payroll. Shaking his head, he delved into his pockets to retrieve a life-saving packet of cigarettes and tried to concentrate on what Pujol was saying. 'As there were no cartridges or spent shells they were probably ordinary hunting rifles and everyone living in the country has at least one in his possession for *la chasse* so Leguyder couldn't identify them.' He took a deep breath. 'The two getaway cars were found at a motorway service station at Beaune first thing this morning, unoccupied of course, and his department will be beavering away all day on your behalf taking them to pieces as soon as they arrive.'

'He told you all that?'

'I think he wanted to impress me, expecting me to forget the details. I don't believe he considers that I'm very bright.'

'The man's a fool.'

Pujol recoiled even further, not realising Pel was referring to Leguyder. 'I thought it would save time if I told you myself,' he said apologetically.

27

'Congratulations,' Pel said dully. 'What about Beaune, did anyone see anything at the service station?'

'Not a thing, sir, Patron,' Pujol stuttered. 'As soon as I saw the fax come through I got on to them and asked. It is assumed that the cars were abandoned during the hours of darkness.'

Pel appreciated the efficiency but not the fact that the general public were usually blind, deaf and remarkably stupid. He didn't think for a minute that anyone could have had the intelligence to realise they were witnessing a group of bandits changing cars, but it would be nice if someone did notice something occasionally.

'What about the insurance companies?'

'Stroppy little sods,' big Bardolle replied, trying hard to keep his foghorn voice down to booming. 'We spent all day on the phone, it was like trying to get water out of a stone, and we came up with nothing. Sorry, Patron, but if the crate was insured independently by the family it wasn't in Montpellier.'

Pel turned to Debray. 'And what have you got to report? And please, try talking French not Chinese, you may understand your computers but sometimes you're a bit tricky to translate, for the juniors,' he added. Debray's reports terrified him. He knew they contained invaluable information but it was often impossible to get at it through the abbreviated computer jargon. On a good day he could be as confusing as Leguyder, on a bad day he was worse.

'Firstly,' Debray said, smiling, 'the preliminary search through the airport personnel has thrown up no fewer than thirty-four possible suspects, but only seven of these have access to the security areas beyond the main public hall and restaurant. There are two men who should be questioned in the security firm in Montpellier and a couple of ex-employees from Blau Beauté. I have all the names and addresses here.' He indicated a depressingly long list. They all knew what it meant: tramping about in the steaming heat interviewing indignant and often difficult citizens, attempting to ferret out that tiny bit of information which might give them the break they needed.

'Secondly,' he continued, 'it's not the first time. In 1992 a helicopter carrying highwaymen stopped a jet on the Corsican runway and got away with ten million francs. They haven't been caught. More recently, in 1996, a jet was held up in Perpignan where the bandits helped themselves to almost five million francs' worth of pesetas.'

'In three words,' Pel pleaded, 'could it be the same gang?'

'In three words: it could be.'

'Get in touch with the men dealing with both cases and see if you can find a common denominator. Collect and collate all the information they can give you, although it may only be a copy-cat crime, you never know.' Pel smoothed his sparse hair and leaned back in his chair; he nearly overbalanced but righted himself just in time. 'There are already one or two interesting factors in this case,' he said, grabbing at the desk in front of him. Finding his Gauloises under his nose he shook one out hurriedly as if it was what he'd intended to do all along. 'Maxine, the daughter, who's been persuaded by her husband to withdraw the reward originally suggested – they have their reasons but in my experience it's out of character. Then the head of the firm, her father, who is too old to travel but not too old to prepare the precious package for transportation. It was him that wanted it to come here – why?' He looked round the room at the expectant faces as he lit up. 'What do we have on the Blau family?'

'So far, not much,' Darcy replied. 'I'm handing that over to de Troq', our impoverished aristocrat. Maxine behaved like a snob and she's got two sisters – he might have more success than us mere mortals.'

'You all know what you're doing,' Pel concluded,

standing up. 'If you don't, come and see me, if you dare. Is there anything else?'

Speeding down the slip road on to the motorway at that moment was a young woman who was pumping desperately on the brake pedal of her old Peugeot 505, but nothing was happening. The driver of a huge lorry in the slow lane realised she was heading straight for him and, knowing it would take time for his long vehicle to come to a stop, he was forced to swerve violently then accelerate as hard as he could into the middle lane to avoid annihilating her. During the manoeuvre his rear end swung just too far out and caught a BMW coming like a bat out of hell up the fast lane, catapulting it off into the central barrier. The lorry driver felt nothing but breathed a sigh of relief at missing the descending 505. As the BMW hit the safety rails and somersaulted over into the traffic coming in the other direction, the driver following it saw the car flying through the air, panicked and wrenched at his steering wheel; he came to an abrupt halt with his bonnet embedded in the back door of the 505. Speeding cars on both carriageways smashed into each other and in a matter of seconds the entire motorway had come to a complete stop. Three people were already dead, half a dozen were seriously injured.

As the sirens roared out of the city towards the lethal tangle, Pel was sitting frowning at his desk. Leguyder had mercifully given up and gone back to his lab, leaving him alone to struggle with the statements taken from the passengers in the hold-up plane. It was quite obvious that the operation had been smooth and professional even to the extent of supplying in-flight entertainment. No one had been touched; only one woman had been frightened, another had been sick through delayed shock, but that was it. The gang had got away with what they came for. It looked like industrial sabotage, perfume pilfering, all this fuss for a few bottles of scent. Something flashed into his memory; scattering paper from his desk like falling leaves on a windy day, he found the pilot's statement and reread the words, 'sacks of potatoes'. An odd way to describe carefully packaged perfume samples, he thought. But they'd got away with them and apparently left nothing except complete chaos at the airport and a monumental headache for Pel. He sifted through the files in his mind for old friends, bandits of the past. Which one of them would be capable of the airport job? There were two possibles, but he was pretty sure neither of them would dare pull something like this on his patch, or would they? Neither of them was behind bars, they'd neatly disappeared – would they risk capture now? He believed them too intelligent to be back dabbling in dishonesty. Disgusted that he was having complimentary thoughts about criminals, Pel removed himself from his chair and strolled round to the other side of his desk to retrieve the fallen papers. He was still on his hands and knees when Annie Saxe, the only female member of his team, knocked on his door and came in with some coffee. Her bright green eyes were smiling at him out of a mane of wild red hair. She was used to her boss; seeing him fight with reports was an everyday occurrence.

'*Décaf?*' she asked gently, placing the mug on his desk.

Looking up from the floor, Pel realised for the first time that her thick curling hair was tumbling over her shoulders. 'Looks more like *décoiff*,' he said, trying to find his scowl. 'Tie your mane back, would you – you'll frighten the outlaws if we ever catch the devils. You look more like an escaped lion than a member of the police force.'

'That's my nickname,' she grinned, 'the Lion of Belfort.'

31

'Still? I thought it disappeared a long time ago when you slowed down to turbo boost and only broke things once a day.'

'It's still with me, although I haven't broken anything for at least a month. Have you heard about the motorway pile-up? Apparently it's bedlam, twisted cars and ambulances everywhere. If I'd been coming in later this morning I would've been in it. Makes you think, doesn't it?'

'It makes me think that it's a damn good thing you weren't,' Pel said, heaving himself to standing position. He sipped idly at his coffee and managed to scald his upper lip; crashing the mug back on to the desk, he slopped small brown stains generously in all directions. He swore decisively and tried again. 'I can't afford to lose a good man at a time like this.'

It was almost a compliment, from Pel it was flattering, and Annie slid out through the door feeling pleased. It had been a long haul from the days when she'd first joined the team but she'd made it. She smiled a secret smile as Cheriff, their stately French-born Arab, passed her in the corridor.

He winked at her. 'I forgot to tell you, with your hair like that you look as if you've just had an energetic lover.'

'You should know,' she grinned happily and left him to knock on Pel's door.

Pel was still shuffling damp papers like a pack of sticky cards and puffing vigorously on a newly lit cigarette. He reminded Cheriff of a studious and very bad-tempered dragon as he gathered up the pile in the lingering smoke. He held it out to the good-looking Arab. 'Do something with that, will you? It doesn't like me,' he said. 'And tell Pujol I'm still waiting for him.'

Cheriff was sure the boss's desire to see his younger colleague hadn't come through to the sergeants' room. 'When did you call for him, Patron?' he asked innocently.

'I haven't yet.'

32

As another siren shot down the street below Pel's window, he sat back and stared at his glowing cigarette end. He was feeling slightly better. He'd unloaded a lot of boring sifting and sorting on to someone else, and the mess on the motorway wasn't his problem. But he was in for a nasty surprise.

3

That evening when he arrived home, Pel's wife was absent – still counting the takings from her string of boutiques, he hoped – but Madame Routy, their fire-eating house-keeper, was in the kitchen, clad in hobnailed boots as usual, judging by the sound of her feet on the hard *carrelage* floor. Pel was about to enter to help himself to a small reviving drink when a resounding clatter of sauce-pans persuaded him he'd be better off strolling round the garden. It was still hot outside, making him more aware of the growing dryness in his throat; determined to get the better of Madame Routy just once, he turned to go back in when he noticed Yves Pasquier sitting on the ter-race of the next-door house. His head was bent in con-centration over something in his hands, a frown wrinkled his young intelligent forehead. Must be studying, Pel thought, but he called to him all the same.

'*Deux secondes*,' Yves replied without looking up. 'Come through the hedge if you like, Pel, we'll have a drink.'

Pel joined his neighbour and sat beside him, straining his neck to see what was so fascinating.

'Sorry,' he said, 'can't stop. About to beat my record.'

Pel patiently waited a full five minutes and just as he was in fear of nodding off in the evening sun, Yves shouted, '*Merde!*' and threw a rectangular plastic box on the table. 'I'll get you that drink now,' he said and went into the kitchen.

While Yves was collecting the necessary bottles and glasses, Pel eyed the grey box. It appeared to have what looked like a screen on it. Modern technology, he sighed, and picked up what he thought was a minuscule television, searching for the on/off switch. However, after trying all the buttons, the only thing that came on to the screen was an assortment of geometric shapes that travelled from top to bottom, piling up on each other and making an erratic pattern.

A cold beer and a long explanation later, Pel slipped back through the hedge to his own garden. In his jacket pocket was the small computer game console that Yves had insisted on lending him.

His wife met him in their *salon* and kissed him lovingly on the cheek. She was clearly pleased to see her husband, which always surprised Pel: he wouldn't have given himself house room.

'Shall we have a little aperitif?' she asked. 'We could enjoy the last of the sun outside.'

'What about supper?' Pel was hungry and worried that his permanent indigestion was going to have to wait.

'Madame Routy tells me it'll be ready in ten minutes, just enough time for a little drink. I don't know about you but I need one, I've been chasing round antique shops all afternoon.' She gently pushed him back outside and went to collect a tray. Pel did as he was told and sat beneath their elegant parasol in a wicker garden seat. They were usually very comfortable, but this evening his was lumpy; putting his hand down to investigate, he discovered the Gameboy in his pocket.

'Stupid thing,' he muttered. He couldn't understand how anyone, particularly anyone of any intelligence, could waste their time playing with such a thing. However, he switched it on. By the time his wife came back out to join him he'd managed painfully to complete one whole line of shapes. Satisfied at his success he switched it off and placed it on the table, turning in his seat to smile at his wife. It frightened most people but not Madame Pel; she smiled contentedly back. He couldn't imagine what she saw in him – he believed that because

35

of vanity she didn't wear her glasses except when working and that she'd never really seen what he looked like, particularly first thing in the morning with his eyes red from sleeping badly and his remaining hair standing on end as if he'd been playing with a badly connected electrical socket. He wasn't a handsome man by any means and he wondered how in hell he'd managed to trap a poor unsuspecting woman, a very attractive woman too, into marrying him. Not only was she attractive but she was kind, intelligent and wealthy. She ran a string of shops in the city, one of which was the famous Nanette's, hairdressers to only the very rich. Although he realised Madame would have gently reprimanded him for describing Nanette's as a simple hairdressers. That was how it had started, but now it was a veritable beauty parlour with massage maniacs, dietitians, dermatologists and every product under the sun to turn a witch covered in warts into a beauty queen. It occurred to him that they also sold perfume.

His smile had slipped a bit and turned into a fully fledged grimace. He redressed it and reached for his drink.

'*Santé*,' he said, but his mind was racing on to other things. 'Could a number of perfume samples look like a sack of potatoes?' he asked suddenly.

Madame wasn't surprised. 'I doubt it,' she said seriously, 'but it depends on the size and shape of the bottles. There is a famous perfume that comes in a round bottle almost the size of your average potato, but it leaves the factory already boxed and wrapped tightly in cellophane paper. The box is square.'

Pel digested the information. 'No,' he went on, 'these were just samples, they hadn't been put on the market yet.'

'Then I would say no. Perfume samples are carefully

sealed in airtight containers, either glass or plastic. Air contaminates perfume, like the light, and after a while it goes off, the smell changes. If they were only samples the manufacturer wouldn't waste money on expensive packaging such as pretty potato-shaped bottles.'

That's what he'd thought. Going on to ask his wife about Blau Beauté, he learnt that it had been started up in the fifties and had been a small but very successful firm. Recently, since the owner had handed over to his daughter, they had been expanding rapidly. They'd lost their exclusiveness because the quality wasn't so high, but in bringing their prices down had gained a great many customers. It was interesting but not really the stuff for industrial sabotage.

His wife, however, was not of the same opinion. 'The beauty trade is a vicious one,' she told him. 'Everyone wants the mystery ingredient to keep us young. You'd be surprised how much women, and gentlemen nowadays, are prepared to spend on creams and lotions. Each company has their secret ingredient and promises miracles, they're very jealous of each other. With perfume it's the same thing. The adverts make believe that with a particular scent we can become sex symbols, and there is great secrecy about its manufacture, particularly just before a launching.'

Pel sat in the sergeants' room the following morning listening glumly to the negative reports his men were giving him. The personnel at the airport had been interviewed and, with the exception of one man, appeared to be innocent. 'And he's not guilty of setting up the robbery of the plane,' Nosjean explained, 'just whipping money from his mates' lockers.'

Cheriff was no more encouraging about the passengers'

statements. 'They all check out,' he said. 'Only the occasional bit of adultery and that doesn't concern us at the moment.'

The men in the security firm at Montpellier had been carefully investigated and so had the two ex-employees of Blau Beauté, but they all looked like dead ends.

'Have Forensics found anything on the two getaway cars yet?'

'There were dog hairs, human hairs, bits of fluff, sweet papers, cigar and cigarette ends, the usual rubbish found in family cars, but nothing to help us so far,' Darcy replied. 'What is unusual, however, is that neither was reported stolen. When we told the owners, we had some difficulty in making them believe it. We had to go to the garages underneath their flats and insist they take a look. You should have seen their confident faces crumple when they found them empty. One was an electrician, the other a plumber, living miles from each other, but they both have vans for work during the week and only use the cars on Saturdays to take their wives shopping and Sundays to go to church. When we left them they were in a state of shock.'

'A carefully worked-out choice,' Pel said. 'Someone had been watching for the right cars for a long time. Get over and see the neighbours this time, find out if anyone was seen hanging around the garages. And what about the vehicle or vehicles they transferred to at Beaune, any news from there?'

There was none, their bandits had vanished into thin air.

'What about the Blau family?'

'The old man lives with Maxine and her husband, Jean-Paul Rolland,' de Troq' replied. 'They live on the edge of a lake near Sète. Josephe Blau is a bit of a mystery. I can find no record of him before 1946 when he arrived on the south coast. He applied his chemist's qualifications to create a cottage industry of beauty creams; since then he's made a fortune and bought a factory. His wife died years ago but they had three daughters. Maxine and her husband are both directors of Blau Beauté. He was studying dermatology and she was a nurse in the burns unit at Avignon hospital – they gave everything up to join the firm in 1986. They have two grown-up children, both girls, both in Canada. The second daughter, Lorette, married a farmer in the Mâcon area; she runs the office of the *vignoble*. They also have two grown-up daughters who have joined their cousins in Canada. Blau's third child, Jacqueline, lives on the outskirts of Ste Etienne; she has no children and is divorced. She runs a smallholding where she raises goats and changes partners frequently, so I'm told. Neither Lorette nor Jacqueline has ever shown any interest in their father's business.'

Darcy followed Pel back to his office with his already thick file. Pel wanted to have another look at the pilot's statement.

'Industrial sabotage,' he said, leafing through the pages. 'There's something that doesn't seem right. If I remember correctly, the pilot said they grabbed the bags and bunged them into the car.'

'Bags of potatoes,' Darcy added, smiling. He'd also picked up on the odd description.

'Exactly,' Pel agreed. 'Perfume samples would have a great deal of difficulty looking like bags of spuds. The bandits knew what they wanted, only bothered to open one cargo compartment and only emptied one crate, so if they'd been perfume samples they would have handled them with more delicacy. And,' he went on, reading through the aircraft's cargo manifest, 'perfume samples packed in polystyrene pellets would not have weighed all that much, and yet when the crate was delivered by the security firm at Montpellier it weighed in at over thirty kilos. That's a hell of a lot of perfume. Maxine was supposed to be there when the old man was doing the packing. I wonder what she's not telling us. I wonder if something was added to the crate.'

'Scrap metal?' Darcy suggested.

Having confirmed the whereabouts of Maxine and her husband by means of a simple telephone call, and satisfied that he wouldn't be interrupted, Pel left Darcy in charge and set off towards the airport with de Troq' just as most people were beginning to think about what to have for lunch.

It was a short but boring flight straight down to the coast and they arrived on the edge of the Mediterranean Sea where the afternoon sun glittered off the water with a brilliance that hurt their eyes. At Sète aerodrome a car was waiting for them and, having consulted his map, de Troq' set off west. Twenty minutes later he drove the car into an avenue of tall pine trees that took them to the edge of a lake. The Blaus' house was a small château, with round towers at each corner and pointed roofs like witches' hats. It was all in excellent repair and the gardens surrounding it looked as if they were cared for by well-paid horticulturists. Jutting out into the smooth water of the lake was a small wooden walkway and on the very end of it was a wheelchair. A thin coil of smoke rose from a shadow sitting in it. The two policemen made their way round the building towards the jetty, but the moment their feet started across the wooden boards a cracked voice stopped them.

'If you try and push me in, I'll shoot you.'

The chair swung round revealing a crumpled old man, his knees covered by a tartan rug, his wispy white hair dancing in the slight breeze. Between his lips was a small cigar, in his shaking hands was a revolver.

'Not another step,' he croaked.

Pel sighed. 'Do your stuff, de Troq',' he said, and left the aristocratic detective to make the presentations.

'So you're not lawyers or thieves?' the old man finally asked, lowering his gun.

'No, sir, we are policemen. We would like to ask you one or two questions about the crate you sent north.'

'None of your business,' he replied. 'All very secret. Not allowed to say a word.'

'Unfortunately it has become our business.'

'Why? What's happened to it?' The old man's eyes were wide with worry.

'It was stolen,' Pel told him bluntly, surprised he didn't already know.

For a moment they thought he was about to have a heart attack, but he recovered his composure and puffed deliberately on his cigar. 'Wheel me into the shade, young man. This sun's too bright, can't see you properly.'

With Pel walking slowly beside him, de Troq' carefully pushed the old man from the jetty and into the shade of a spacious courtyard.

'Ah, now I see you. What's all this nonsense about my crate, then? Might as well admit it as you seem to know all about it anyway. It should have been safely in the bank by now.'

Pel had the unpleasant duty of telling Blau exactly what had happened, watching the old man's shock turn to anger then sadness. He sat staring at them through half-closed eyes, hating them for the news they brought.

He said nothing but looked away across the shining lake as if searching for something or someone. He sighed deeply and turned his weary eyes back towards the two policemen.

41

'Damn them and damn you. Take me inside. I want a drink.'

In spite of the intense heat outside, the small room he invited them into was cool. The change of temperature was refreshing, although for a moment they all blinked hard, blinded by the sudden darkness.

It was a kitchen cum library. A stone sink was carved into one thick wall and an old stove stood beside it; the other three walls were covered in well-stocked bookshelves. One further piece of furniture was placed in the middle of the room: a well-used table with ornate legs.

'This is what they call my playroom,' he said, putting the revolver carefully on the table. 'It's where they put me when the weather's nice and they don't have to lock me away in modern comfort upstairs. I have a lift, you see, that takes me up and down to my apartment – it's behind that fine oak door. In the winter they disconnect it so I can't get out, but in the summer I'm allowed out to play and dream.'

'What do you dream of, monsieur?'

'Nothing, not now, except the golden peace of death. Here, young man, go to the bookshelf over there and remove the twin leather-bound volumes at the end of my encyclopaedia shelf. There's a bottle of good cognac hidden behind them. We'll have a drop to take away the bitter taste of theft.'

As de Troq' handed him the bottle, the old man pulled off his rug and stood up. 'Treat me like a blooming cripple,' he said angrily and began his search for glasses, 'just because I've had a couple of tumbles. Anyone would think I was losing my marbles the way they speak to me. Still got my brain.' He tapped his temple, making the fine crystal tinkle in his bony hands.

Pel let him pour and waited until they had all tasted the velvety liqueur before asking his next question.

42

'Your daughter, Maxine, didn't tell you about the robbery, monsieur. Would you know why?'

'She thinks she knows everything but she never tells me anything. My wife was the same.'

'What was in the crate?'

'Don't you know?'

'I'd like you to tell me,' Pel said.

He thought for a moment before replying. 'Perfume.'

'I think there may have been something else as well.'

'Go and ask Maxine – she'll tell you,' he went on confidently. 'She was there when I was packing it up.'

'Yes, I know, and she too said it was perfume, but I wonder if an addition was made before it left the factory?'

'Why do you wonder that?'

'The crate weighed too much,' Pel said simply.

'How do you know what perfume weighs? It was a big box, with lots of padding to protect the bottles.'

'The box and the polystyrene padding weighed no more than a few kilos, monsieur, unless it was made of cast iron, which it was not. The rest was removed but I don't think there'd have been enough room for nearly thirty kilos of perfume – it would have been a mighty big bottle.'

'Must have been a mix-up,' Blau said cheerfully. 'You must have got the wrong box. I sent perfume,' but he was drowning his sorrow in another cognac. It was a possibility: the box could have been switched accidentally or deliberately before arriving at Montpellier airport. But that would mean that the hold-up in Burgundy was nothing to do with the Blaus and also that nobody knew what had been stolen, except the bandits. Had they had a nasty surprise when opening the sacks? Pel sighed: it was getting unpleasantly complicated.

Monsieur Blau sat heavily down in the wheelchair again, tears coursing down his cheeks, mumbling to

43

himself. 'No point in carrying on now, my life's caught me up and paid me back.' Pel and de Troq' watched the old man fading away in front of them. He shook his head to their questions and said very little that was coherent. They wanted to know why he'd chosen their city to hide the samples, but he replied, 'For safety,' his voice faltering over the words. Shakily he took another mouthful of cognac. 'The future, my family . . .' he muttered.

Finally they pushed him out on to a terrace shaded by a pergola dripping sweet-smelling roses and weren't surprised to find he'd fallen asleep. De Troq' slipped back into his playroom to replace the bottle behind the books and rinse the three glasses in the sink.

As they drove away Pel was thinking hard. 'De Troq',' he said, 'I may be wrong and he really did ship the perfume, but his reactions were odd.'

'It was his life's work,' de Troq' pointed out.

'Only part of his life's work, there's still everything else they produce, the creams and lotions. The perfume was Maxine's idea,' Pel corrected. 'But there's more to it than that. He was mumbling about his life catching him up and paying him back. Dig deeper into his past. You might find something – you never know, miracles do happen.'

'It would also be interesting to find Mariette of St Beauzile.'

Pel turned under the safety belt to look at de Troq'. '*Raconte*,' he said.

'The two leather-bound volumes behind which he hides his cognac,' de Troq' explained. 'They were original copies of *Mémoires sur l'Histoire de la France*,' he said, negotiating a roundabout. 'It's rather a saucy account of French life in the royal courts. They were both given to him with love by Mariette of St Beauzile in 1945.'

'St Beauzile isn't far from our beloved city . . .' Pel reached for his cigarettes. ' . . . the delivery point of the crate.'

44

De Troq' changed gear and drew up outside the aerodrome. 'Something else that's interesting, Patron,' he said, climbing out and locking the car. 'A lot of the books on the shelves weren't in French. It occurred to me that maybe he's not. During the war the Germans gave Jewish refugees new names – *schwarz* for instance, it means black, *weiss* for white, *blau* for blue.'

When Pel arrived in his office that evening, weary from the journey and the heat, there was bad news. It was the pile-up on the motorway. It wasn't simply idiots driving too fast, it was worse, far worse.

4

'The brake fluid had been drained from the key car,' Leguyder told him. 'There wasn't a drop in it.'

Pel, who knew nothing about cars, asked if it was necessarily deliberate.

'If I'm sitting here, wasting my precious time,' the scientist retorted, 'it's because I am certain the fluid was drained off deliberately in order to cause harm or even death to the driver of the car concerned.'

'A mistake?' Pel offered. 'Someone servicing the car who forgot to refill the reservoir?'

'Hardly. When the reservoir reaches danger point a warning light comes on on the dashboard. It had been disconnected under the bonnet. Having found that, we started looking behind the wheels at the rubber tubing – it had been pierced with a sharp instrument, for example a darning needle. The hole was almost invisible and wouldn't have had much effect while the car was stationary or moving forward, but the moment the driver used the brakes the Lockheed fluid would have poured out. Eventually the reservoir was emptied and the brakes were rendered useless.'

'You're saying, then, that it was attempted murder?'

'Congratulations,' Leguyder said sarcastically, 'ten out of ten. However, the driver of that particular car was lucky and she survived. Although she'll be wearing a surgical collar round her neck for a couple of weeks, she won't be undergoing surgery or hospitalisation for any length of time, unless of course she falls down the stairs in the next twenty-four hours, which is always possible with your clients.'

*

While Angelface Aimedieu and Annie rushed off to interview Mariline Philibert, the young woman who had been driving the car with the drained brakes, Pel was thinking about the old man Blau. When they'd arrived at the château he'd threatened to shoot them if they tried to push him into the water. It bothered Pel, it wasn't the normal behaviour of an elderly man sitting soaking up the afternoon sun in a wheelchair. Wily old peasants often pointed a rifle out of a window before answering the door, but Blau's gun had been a small handgun, the sort carried by maniacs in American films or maybe the Maquis during the war. A gun left over from the Resistance? He shouted into the intercom for de Troq'.

'I'm pretty sure it was a Browning automatic,' he was told.

'And?' Pel was waiting for more.

'And although there aren't many of that age around nowadays, there were plenty dropped into France on the ends of British parachutes for use by the Resistance during the war. He could have picked it up almost anywhere.'

'At Beauzile, for instance,' Pel suggested.

'It's possible,' de Troq' agreed. 'Burgundy was well and truly occupied. It also had an active underground movement against the Germans.'

'Could that be the part of his life that's catching him up and paying him back?'

'I've been in touch with the Mairie at St Beauzile, Patron. Unfortunately their records for the war years were destroyed, and after that there is nothing on Blau, so I tried Sète. They have the same problem with incomplete documents before 1945, but the Mayor's secretary did find a marriage registered between Josephe Blau, resident of that city, and Jeanne-Marie, a local shopkeeper, in 1947. Almost immediately afterwards they went into business together and Blau Beauté was born.'

47

'His expertise, her premises,' Pel added. 'What does Maxine have to say on her father's past?'

'Not much, she was distinctly unhelpful. She said rather loudly that the Germans had a lot to answer for and her father was lucky to survive. She also forbade us to upset him with stupid questions that would bring back painful memories.'

'So your theory of Blau being a name given to him during the occupation looks correct. The Germans robbed him of his identity and his past and now he's been robbed of the future for his family – that's what he said, isn't it?' but Pel continued before de Troq' had a chance to reply, 'Did she tell you why her father knew nothing about the robbery of the crate? Or why he protects himself with an old Browning?'

'I didn't mention that we'd been to see him.'

'Perhaps it's just as well. Maxine is also a suspect – we don't want her pushing him in the lake before we get this mess sorted out.'

As Pel was collecting his paraphernalia, Gauloises, lighters and more Gauloises, in preparation for his journey home, Aimedieu and Annie came in to tell him that Mariline Philibert couldn't think of anyone who would want to kill her by emptying the brake fluid out of her car – in fact she'd been amazed at the idea. She was a simple student at the university trying to make ends meet by working as a *pionne* at the *lycée*.

Pel decided it was time to leave the office.

When he arrived the next morning, he slammed the door to his office shut and a sheet of paper wafted off his desk, floating gently to the floor. He bent to pick it up as Darcy came in.

'Ah, I see you've found the message I left you,' he said, dazzling Pel with his Prince Charming smile. 'Monsieur

Blau said it was urgent, he wants to speak to you personally about finding his crate. He said he was willing to pay the reward personally.'

Pel glanced at the message then laid it carefully on his desk again. 'How did he sound?' he asked.

'Old and frightened.'

'Did he say anything else?'

'He wasn't terribly easy to understand, he was slurring his words rather badly.'

'Obviously been reading the *Mémoires sur l'Histoire de la France* again.'

'Patron?'

'It doesn't matter. Where's de Troq'?'

'Not in yet.'

'As soon as he arrives tell him to – No, you make the call. Get through to the old boy as fast as possible. I'd like to hear what he has to say myself.'

While Pel lit up, sat down and started turning pages in the fast-growing Blau family file, Darcy tapped the appropriate numbers into Pel's telephone.

After a minute or two Darcy clasped his hand over the receiver. 'Maxine wants to speak to you,' he said.

'Right now I don't want to speak to her, and if she's there I can't talk to the old man either,' Pel replied. 'Make an excuse and ring off.'

'I think you'd better take the call, Patron, the old man's disappeared.'

Maxine Blau was in a state, almost hysterical. Pel found it difficult to make head or tail of what she was telling him. Eventually, through ill-practised patience, he calmed her down.

'But my father's gone,' she yelled. 'When we came home last night he wasn't here.'

'What time did you arrive home, madame?'

'I can't remember, it was late and there was no sign of him, except three of my best glasses had been washed up and placed on the draining board. And it wasn't him that did that, he never washes anything, he must have had visitors. He's been kidnapped!'

'Why do you think that?'

'Well, it's possible isn't it? The police who came last night thought so.'

'Again, madame, I ask you why? That's to say, what would the kidnappers have to gain?'

'We're a rich family, Chief Inspector Pel, I would suggest they'd be after rather a lot of money.'

'You'd better give me the name of the inspector in charge of the case and I'll get on to him.'

'Things are hotting up,' he said, putting the phone down. 'Take the morning meeting yourself, I've got another call to make. And Darcy,' he added, 'Aimedieu and Annie have got to do better with the motorway smash, tell them to use their imagination. Tell them to try Pujol, his imagination is unbelievable, but sometimes, I repeat, sometimes he's worth listening to.'

Pel got through to the police at Sète and, after being passed from one office to another, at last found himself talking to an obstreperous but important policeman.

'I hope it's important,' he shouted. 'I have no time for fools!'

'Police work is always important,' Pel pointed out, 'and I'm Chief Inspector Pel calling from Burgundy. My men do not dare consider me to be a fool.'

The Commissaire apologised. 'I thought I was still talking to the desk sergeant. He's a prize idiot. What can I do to help?'

They talked through the circumstances of the Blau kidnapping until Pel suggested the possibility of murder.

'Murdered! Why would anyone murder a poor old bloke like Blau?'

Pel explained the family's connection with the airport hold-up and the possibility that someone wanted to keep him quiet for ever about the mix-up or the secret ingredient if there was one. 'He rang last night,' he said. 'I wasn't here, but my second-in-command took the message. He says Monsieur Blau seemed frightened and was most anxious to recover the contents of the crate. It's possible he has an idea as to who stole it.'

In a cloud of smoke from a newly lit cigarette Pel burst in on the morning meeting. 'And I want someone to find out about the other two Blau daughters, in detail,' he bellowed. 'Their work contacts, indiscretions if they have any, and let's face it, they're only human – although you wonder when you see that painted face hiding the mind of a computer. Perhaps Maxine's just a well-programmed robot. But be careful,' he added. 'I don't want her knowing she's under suspicion for even picking her pretty nose for the moment.'

He left the occupants of the sergeants' room feeling windswept and happily settled himself once again behind his own desk, trying to untangle his ideas – but he knew ideas were not enough, they needed good hard facts and of those they had very few. With his brain in overdrive he picked up the phone, lit another life-saving Gauloise and dialled Cousin Roger's number. He was the only member of his wife's family he liked and they'd often enjoyed an illicit cigarette in the garden discussing the imbeciles that ruled the world, while the rest of the family pretended not to notice. He was a city accountant and could sometimes acquire snippets of information about business transactions where a policeman would come up against brick walls of silence.

As usual Roger was delighted to hear from Pel. As usual Pel was surprised. Roger came to the point quickly and asked Pel what he wanted; to make a change, Pel invited him for a drink after work.

'So telling me what you want will be more confidential or because the heat's getting to you and you're thirsty?'

'Both,' Pel admitted. 'I may be barking up the wrong tree entirely and I don't want to upset those concerned, or put them on their guard if I'm right. Also because police in another region are involved and I shouldn't be poking around in their territory without them knowing.'

Stubbing out his cigarette, Pel rose from his chair and strolled round his desk to the window. A simple hold-up at the airport was bad enough, but one that involved family histrionics was enough to make a man worry rats. He passed a hand through the remains of his hair and stared down into the street. He could see his men charging off in all directions preparing themselves to seek, gather and interpret information. They were a good set of blokes, really, even Annie was a good bloke – it was hard to find someone to take out his wrath on nowadays. Misset, their fading James Bond, was always the favourite choice, but since his mother-in-law had come to live with his family he spent a great deal of extra time in the office, keeping his head down and hiding behind his ridiculous dark glasses in the hope that no one would notice he was there. For the most part he was ignored as being more trouble than he was worth. Pel suspected Annie of giving the typists lessons in self-defence because Misset spent less and less time worrying them too, or perhaps he was just getting old. Poor old devil. Holy Mother of God! He was five years younger than Pel. That was it, he'd take no more excuses from Misset.

Turning rapidly he swept the phone into his hand. 'Where's Misset?' he demanded.

'Here, Patron,' Misset said, shuffling in through the door.

'What are you doing?'

'About to leave with Darcy for Beaune service station,

52

to see about the two stolen vehicles used as getaway cars in the airport hoist.'

'Heist, Misset, heist,' Pel said despairingly.

Darcy joined them, the sun shining off his thick lustrous black hair. Pel could have killed him.

'Just off, Patron. Here's the list of who's doing what. De Troq's still digging into the Blau family, Debray's playing on his computers and Rigal's manning the phones.' He dropped a sheet of paper on to his boss's desk, did a smart about-turn and marched Misset from the office. Pel glanced at the handwritten list.

Big Bardolle and little Pujol had gone to see Lorette Blau, wife of François Baron, *vigneron* in Mâcon. Nosjean, the tired Napoleon, had gone to check the airport and security firm personnel with Brochard. Cheriff and Didier Darras were hunting down Jacqueline Blau amongst her goats and her changing partners, while Angelface Aimedieu and Annie were hoping to jog the memory of Mariline Philibert, student and survivor of the drained brakes.

Pel nodded, satisfied they were all well occupied. Hoping they'd bring in some results before long, he wandered off deep in thought to see what de Troq' and Debray had cooked up.

The two of them were sitting in front of the infernal computer screen, Debray shaking his right hand as if something nasty was sticking to it.

'What is it?' Pel asked, coming up behind them and assuming they'd discovered the answer to all his problems. He was puffing hard on the inevitable Gauloise and looked like a steam train negotiating a siding.

'Cramp,' Debray answered.

His hopes dashed, Pel glared at de Troq' who immediately stood up: his aristocratic upbringing was occasionally irritating to Pel who felt like an uneducated tramp in his presence. 'There are no Mariettes at all in Beauzile,' he reported. 'One or two in the surrounding countryside, but none the right age to have known Blau in 1945. However, I've also spoken to the Mayor's office again – they've managed to find a badly burnt document concerning that year. It states that the château there was occupied for eight months before the Germans pulled out and there was a Polish refugee working the land, name of Nowak, changed to Blau by the occupiers. This may be his missing past. I think it would be worth a trip to see the *curé* – I'm told that although he's retired he still lives in the village. The new priest says he's very deaf and has no phone, but a memory like a history book.'

'Get the car,' Pel said. 'I'm coming with you.'

As the heat was suffocating outside, de Troq' suggested taking his own car and leaving the roof down. Baron Charles Henry Victor de Troquereau de Turenne – what a mouthful, it was worse even than Evariste Clovis Désiré Pel. Ambitious parents should be more careful when choosing names for their children, although Pel wouldn't have minded being a baron. In fact a simple countship would have done, he thought to himself. He sighed . . . but he'd probably have ended up being a policeman anyway – de Troq' was. An impoverished baron who had to gallop around in the midday sun with his balding boss. Impoverished aristocrats were a mystery to Pel. How could he be impoverished, he wondered, and drive a car as big as a battleship with a leather strap over its bonnet and headlamps as large as lighthouses? Perhaps poverty was relative, like most things. He settled himself into the leather upholstery and checked that his safety belt was done up properly. Pel was a bad driver and an appalling passenger. However, de Troq' was well aware of Pel's phobia about fast drivers and took it nice and slowly, easing his bus out into the city traffic and heading north-west towards Beauzile.

It was a pleasant trip with the warm wind whispering in their ears as they cruised through the countryside. Burgundy, the promised land, the only place to live ... Pel watched it flash past. It was looking beautiful. The vast wheat fields on either side of the road were already deep gold, reflecting the summer sun, and the peasants, usually grim-faced and bad-tempered with intruders in their area, waved gaily as they passed. Most of them were women and the idea occurred to Pel that perhaps it had something to do with the magnificent car being driven by a handsome young man. It was a shame he was there to spoil it.

The neatly painted houses of Beauzile nestled round the pretty church which sat proudly on the highest point of the village. In the middle of the tidy square was a memorial to the men lost in the war, but the place had a feeling of life about it; clean white washing flapped lazily in the small well-kept gardens and bright red geraniums hung from every window sill. Behind the half-closed shutters someone was playing the piano exquisitely, the notes dancing between the pale stone buildings. When they'd walked a few paces towards the only bar, a couple of dogs came tearing down the street, attacked each other savagely then sped off again in the opposite direction. It was all very normal.

They found Monsieur le Curé's house and as they knocked at the priest's door the piano playing stopped. After a long wait they heard someone shuffling towards the front of the house; at last the door opened and a pair of bent wire spectacles perched precariously on the end of a long thin nose stared out at them. His beady black eyes, like two polished marbles, studied their identification. Satisfied with their credentials, he struggled to haul open the heavily studded oak door, catching his voluminous robes on the enormous key and tripping over his walking stick several times. He showed them down a long dark corridor towards a square of light and, stepping gingerly over the threshold, took them into a small courtyard filled with sunshine and warmth.

'Sit yourselves down,' he said and toppled into a large armchair under a mulberry tree. 'This is my secret garden,' he explained, waving his stick in a circle and nearly removing Pel's nose. 'Only now have I time to listen to the hum of summer and smell the enchanted perfume from my flowers, now that it's almost too late.'

An equally bent old housekeeper staggered out and placed a tray with carafe and glasses on the metal table between them.

'You're a good girl,' he said to her gently patting her behind as she turned to leave. 'Thank you.'

With shaking hands he served them iced lemon squash then watched them carefully as they tasted it. 'Good, isn't it? I make it myself from local lemons. In the winter I drink it hot with a drop of rum. Gets the old circulation going, don't you know. Now, what is it you wanted to ask me?'

Communication was hazardous, Pel not wishing to shout in case ears were straining behind the open windows looking down on to the courtyard, and Monsieur le Curé insisting that he spoke up, being virtually stone deaf. Eventually, however, the message got through and the priest sighed. 'Ah, yes,' he said, 'Mariette.'

'You know her?'

'Indeed, it is very hot, help yourself to some more lemon.'

Pel tried again a little more loudly. 'No,' came the reply, 'I don't know Mariette, but a lot of interest is being shown in her. Last month a young woman, almost a child, came to see me, asking about my parishioners, and as recently as two weeks ago a gentleman wanted to know about her.

Now two policemen. I ask myself what Mariette has been up to.'

'If we could locate her, we might be able to find out. We believe she knew a man called Nowak or Blau, who was at the château during the occupation.'

'Ah, yes,' he said, scratching his chin, 'that would be the refugee. It was the German colonel who changed his name, you know.'

'So he was here?'

'Oh, yes. He worked the land, growing vegetables and looking after the pigs. Food was difficult at that time for all of us. The Germans took everything, there was little left for us.' He closed his eyes as if it helped his memory. 'I have to admit my part in the Resistance against them,' he said. 'There must have been good men among them but we didn't see any. War does strange things to human beings, no one behaves normally, not even the priest of the village. I shot at one, you see – he was whipping a child no more than seven years old because she'd stuck her tongue out at him. I missed, of course, and was badly beaten for my trouble, but the little girl got away.'

For a short time the old man reminisced about the years long past. They'd been lucky in their village, the horrors had been kept to a minimum and fifty years had healed many wounds, but Pel and de Troq' knew nothing was forgiven, nothing was forgotten, that would take at least another fifty years. Pel had only been five years old when the war ended but he remembered the fear his parents had instilled in him about the strangers living in their village. De Troq' was born twenty years later but he knew his grandparents had been robbed of everything except their dignity.

Leaving the past to one side, Pel asked the priest if he knew who the two people were who'd been asking about

57

Mariette. He had to repeat the question twice and at last he was understood.

'The young woman, Lillie she called herself, was researching the modern history of Burgundy. Didn't sound too good a story to me but I listened politely and told her that unfortunately I couldn't help. The gentleman introduced himself as Monsieur Lafage. He claimed Mariette was a long-lost aunt and his mother wanted to make peace with her sister before dying. Another lot of cobblers, of course, and he got the same reply. Mariette doesn't exist; she never was and still isn't here in this diocese.'

'Did you tell the man about the girl's visit?'

'I don't think I mentioned it but I may have. Silly, isn't it – I can remember clearly what happened all that time ago, but I forget what happened yesterday.'

'Can you remember what they looked like?'

'She was quite pretty but too thin and he was ordinary looking.' It was as much as they'd expected.

Pel said very little during the journey back to the city. The old *curé* had been charming but of little help. They knew Blau had been the Polish refugee working at the château at Beauzile. They didn't know who Mariette was. They didn't know why the crate had been sent from the coast to Burgundy, although they suspected he'd had a friendship if not a love affair with the mysterious Mariette. They did know they weren't the only ones after Mariette.

As de Troq' pulled the huge old car to a stop at the first traffic light of the city, Pel finally spoke. 'Someone else has seen that inscription in the books,' he said. 'They too, probably out of curiosity, looked Beauzile up on the map and when Blau started talking about sending his box of samples up here it made them think a lot harder about our Mariette. Trouble is, it could have been any member of the family, the cleaner, the

58

gardener or his wife if he has one.' He sighed. 'De Troq',
any minute now I shall be cancelling all leave and
swallowing ulcer pills. It doesn't look like this is going to
be fun.'

5

That evening Pel relaxed to the dulcet tones of Madame Routy crashing about in the kitchen; she was stirring her cauldron and it made Pel want to leave home. He picked up the Gameboy and went into the garden. Five lines! He looked up, pleased with himself, and Yves Pasquier noticed from the next-door terrace.

'Told you you'd become addicted,' he called, grinning.

'It's a stupid game,' Pel retorted, putting it down.

Yves came through the hole in the hedge carrying two bottles of beer. 'No, it's not,' he said, 'it's logic. Every piece fits, given that your brain works fast enough to locate the right place in the puzzle.'

'Sounds like police work,' Pel said miserably.

'I suppose so. How many lines have you managed?'

Pel showed him while Yves unscrewed the bottles. 'When you get to fifty you should start at a higher level.'

'A higher level?' Pel asked. Like all computer operators Yves was talking gibberish.

'There are nine levels, increasing in speed and therefore in difficulty. I've got to 161 lines starting at level nine.'

Pel slumped in his chair. 'And I thought I was doing so well,' he said.

While Pel was struggling with the Gameboy, Nosjean was pacing the carpet filled with anxiety. Mijo had escaped to do some shopping and Nosjean was left holding the baby. It was terrifying. Chasing criminals, putting up with Pel, even being shot at was less frightening than looking after his six-month-old daughter. Every time he put her down she cried, when he picked her up she belched and spat sour milk on to his shoulder; in the steaming heat of the airless apartment he was beginning to smell like a very old cow that was going off at a rate of knots. There was no air-conditioning in their block of flats and he was suffocating – he longed for a cold beer out on the balcony and to put his aching feet up to watch the park opposite. The baby was damp and sticky. He held her at arm's length and took a good look at her: puce in the face and covered in wool from head to foot, no wonder she was miserable, he was perspiring freely under a short-sleeved cotton shirt.

When Mijo came through the door panting under the weight of her full carrier bags she found her husband outside with his feet up on the railings sucking on a bottle of beer and their almost naked daughter happily cradled against him sucking on a bottle of water. And Nosjean was smoking! The evening started going downhill immediately.

Darcy and Kate had barbecued *merguez* out in front of their remote house, demolishing a cheap bottle of *mousseux* while the spicy sausages spat behind them. The two boys galloped back down the forest track with Rasputin, their monster dog. All three of them were drenched and while they stripped off their dripping clothes, letting them drop into the dust, the boys gaily told their amused mother they'd been swimming in the *lavoir* until a snake had decided to join them. Later, when the meal had been devoured and they disappeared to bed, Darcy and Kate enjoyed their coffee under a vast oak. The surrounding forest was quiet. Not a breath of wind disturbed the branches of the tall trees; just the occasional cry of the buzzards overhead broke the silence.

'This is what the end of a hard day should be like,'

Darcy said contentedly, 'sitting here with you dreaming of what we'll be doing after lights out.' After years of chasing gorgeous girls round the city he'd finally met his match. Kate made him sing, he ached for her, longed for her touch – he even enjoyed her two over-lively sons, most of the time. In fact, thinking about it, he wouldn't mind having one of his own.

'Have you seen Mijo recently?' he asked innocently.

'Not for a week or two. She seems a very anxious mother, doing everything by the book.'

'Nosjean isn't too impressed with fatherhood either.'

'She should relax, let it happen.'

'Would you?'

'What?'

'Relax and let it happen.'

'That depends what *it* is.'

'Having my child.'

'Darcy!' But although she sounded shocked Kate was well aware of Darcy's yearning to procreate.

'I want to be your husband,' he said seriously, 'I want to be your husband and have you all my life.'

He sat up suddenly and looked at her, then slowly repeated what he'd said. *'Je veux devenir ton mari et t'avoir toute ma vie.'*

'Yes.' Kate laughed. 'I got the message the first time.'

'No, it's not that,' Darcy replied. 'Listen, *"mari et t'avoir"*. If you heard that in a different context it could be *"Marie est à voir"*, Marie is to be seen, or even *"Mariette avoir"*.'

'Which doesn't mean a lot.'

'But the name, Mariette, it makes the name Mariette.'

Early the following morning Pel was going through his men's reports again. They gave him no hint as to where they should try next. The vehicles the bandits had transferred to still hadn't been identified and the contents of the crate hadn't turned up. The armed guards who'd taken the box away from Blau Beauté had been thoroughly investigated and had themselves delivered it from the Blau factory; the old man had escorted it in person, tottering along behind them with Maxine holding on to his arm, safely to the aircraft. They'd been in constant radio communication with their office and hadn't stopped *en route*. So what was stolen was what the old man had packed up, the boxes hadn't been changed or mixed up. It was back to Monsieur Blau, and the news on him wasn't good – there was none, which meant he was still missing. The Sète police had been thorough in their search to the extent of dragging the lake in front of the Blau-Rolland château. They'd turned up half a dozen rusty bikes, half a bedstead and an impressive collection of bottles, but no old man.

The owners of the two getaway cars were still nonplussed and had nothing to add; as far as they were concerned there had been no one hanging around their garages and no one had been asking questions about how often their cars were used. The neighbours confirmed it. It amazed Pel: if it was a question of who slept with whom, a bit of cosy adultery, everyone knew about it, and if they didn't they'd make it up, but ask the same people if they'd seen a stranger hanging about day after day, the average reaction was two blank eyes in a face registering a large question mark. But nonetheless the locks had been cut by the same cutters used in the hold-up, the cars taken and the garages relocked with fresh *cadenas*.

Then there was the pile-up on the motorway. Aimedieu and Annie had pestered an absent-minded professor at the university and had come away knowing no more than before except that Mademoiselle Philibert was taking a degree in history and was a conscientious student.

The two Blau sisters, Lorette and Jacqueline, knew

nothing about their father's business and didn't want to talk about him. He was in their opinion a silly old fool. Maxine, however, they said was a greedy bitch. The only extra information his men had unearthed that was of any interest was that all three girls were adopted.

'What's the difference?' Pel asked de Troq' when he was told. He lit a much-needed Gauloise and inhaled deeply. Darcy came through the door, his smile shining as if Walt Disney junior had polished it personally.

'What do you want?' Pel growled.

'Mariette.'

'What about her? Apparently she doesn't exist.'

Darcy explained rapidly. 'It could be a nickname for Blau's girlfriend when he was still a shy refugee. If he'd been trying to say something romantic to her and she was correcting his French, insisting on the liaison between the words, he might just have picked up on it and christened her Mariette.'

'Seems a bit slim,' Pel pointed out, 'but it's possible I suppose. Now all you've got to do is find out which old lady – because Blau's lover will be ancient like him – in Beauzile had a romance with the Polish gardener at the château. Simple really,' he said, 'the sort of thing any Frenchwoman would be willing to admit. Particularly now, fifty years later, when the poor old dear is probably a white-haired grandmother looking forward to a short period of peace and quiet before she finally snuffs it. However, when you've got nothing better to do, you can follow it up.

'For the moment,' Pel went on, 'I'd like you to accompany me to Mariline Philibert's place. The death toll from the motorway pile-up has risen to five now and as we've ground to a halt for the time being on the airport hold-up, it would be satisfying to clear something up. I'd like to know why her brakes were drained, if there is a why. If there isn't a why, our clever little devil might have done it for kicks and therefore may just be thinking of doing it again, and we can't have that, can we?'

She was a pretty young woman, twenty years old with long dark hair and pale blue eyes. She received them into a tiny flat where there were papers and books strewn on every surface. With a smile she apologised for the mess and offered to make them some instant coffee.

Pel asked his questions, to which she shook her head. 'I can't think of anyone who'd want to kill me,' she told them. 'I find it incredible that it was deliberate. Are you absolutely sure?'

'Mademoiselle,' Pel replied patiently, 'I am sure or I wouldn't have come here to ask you. Someone drained the brake fluid from your car with the intention of causing you harm. Help us find the idiot before he tries again either with you or with someone else.'

'Someone else?'

'Perpetrators of crime get a taste for what they do. Once they start it's hard to stop, except by arresting them.'

Mariline was stirring her coffee, a frown crumpling her forehead. 'Look,' she said hesitantly, 'I'm a single student, I go out with guys, occasionally they have wives. They don't tell me at first but when I find out I dump them, I'm not ready for that sort of game. I dumped someone a couple of weeks ago for that very reason – you don't think it could be him, do you?'

'Or his wife?' Darcy suggested.

'Oh come on, she knew nothing about us, we'd only seen each other a couple of times.'

'Mademoiselle Philibert, anything is possible. Please tell us his name.'

'But I don't want to cause trouble, or have anything more to do with him. I didn't really want to go out with him in the first place but he insisted and for the sake of a

65

decent meal in a proper restaurant I finally accepted. But he was much older than me and dead boring, so the second time I ditched him, once I'd finished eating, of course. He was ever so nice about it, said he understood and all that. He paid for the meal, shook my hand and I haven't seen him since.'

'We'll be very discreet with our enquiries,' Pel reassured her.

'Okay . . . well, if you promise.'

'His name.'

'He said he was a baron, so I jokingly called him Milord.'

As soon as they got back to the Hôtel de Police, Pel called de Troq' to his office and asked him how many barons there were in Burgundy.

'Not many,' de Troq' replied, 'and one of them's me.'

'Find out exactly, will you, and bring me the list as soon as you have it.'

It didn't take long for Debray's computer to print out the short list of nobility in Burgundy and, as de Troq' pointed out to Pel, he was the only one under the age of sixty-five; this was due to the fact that his father had died in a hunting accident when he was still at school.

'De Troq',' Pel sighed, 'I hate to ask you this, but have you ever been out with Mariline Philibert?'

'Never heard of her until she got wiped off the road and I don't think Véronique would be too pleased if I had.'

'Véronique?'

'Véronique de Maistre-Ricard. Our families have been negotiating our marriage for some time now and for once I'm encouraging them. Wedding bells are highly probable, Patron.'

Pel managed a fatherly smile before turning it quickly

into his more usual scowl. 'And what about Darcy? When's he going to make an honest woman out of the delicious Kate?'

'You'll have to ask him,' de Troq' answered diplomatically, 'but at least he's not a baron and therefore nothing to do with Mariline.'

Pel scratched his chin as he leaned back in his chair. 'So Mariline's boyfriend wasn't a real baron.'

'It's a good way to catch a girl though, claiming to be titled. It could be his surname,' de Troq' suggested. 'There are quite a few of them about, and it isn't unknown for them to use the name to their advantage. You know, Jean-Louis Baron, of 2 rue de la Gare, Chalon, becomes Jean-Louis, Baron of Chalon, and strictly speaking it's true. In fact I noticed one of the Blau daughters is married to François Baron, the *vigneron* in Mâcon.'

Pel held his breath, wondering if this could be it. He called Bardolle and Pujol into his office the moment they arrived at midday.

'Tell me about Lorette Blau and her husband,' he demanded. 'For the moment I'm particularly interested in the husband.'

It turned out however that, although Bardolle and Pujol had seen the manager of the vineyard, it was only after much insistence that they'd finally been allowed into the office to talk to Lorette.

'She was surprised at the news of her father's disappearance,' big Bardolle said, 'but had no useful information as regards where he could have disappeared to. We also told her that the airport hold-up concerned a valuable package belonging to her father's firm and she said she had never had anything to do with the family business and wasn't about to start now. She asked her man, the manager, to see us off the property. I nearly belted the bloke one.'

Pel raised his eyebrows. 'Obnoxious little sod he was,'

67

Bardolle continued, 'full of hot air and pomposity, and', he added, 'he was black.'

'It's a good thing you didn't,' Pel said. 'With your strength you'd have been had up for grievous bodily harm and that would be standing on your head with one hand tied behind your back. Belting blokes is not normally advised in the course of duty, especially if they're not white, you know what the Race Relations Board is like. Thump anyone, but not one of our friends with a distinguished tan, ask Cheriff your coloured colleague, he'll tell you all about it, he's sick to the back teeth at not being treated like a normal human being.'

'She wasn't very nice either,' Pujol interjected cautiously.

Pujol the Puppy was a new young member of Pel's team and although in the first few weeks Pel was to be heard shouting at him to go back to his basket to lick his wounds, they'd since learnt that he kept his eyes and ears open, often noticing tiny details the others could miss. He had an overactive imagination which could be extremely irritating but once in a blue moon it turned out to be cause for excitement. Pel suspected his idea of 'not very nice' was the understatement of the year.

'In what way', he asked, 'was she not very nice?'

Pujol backed off, expecting a storm of his boss's impatience. 'Well,' he said slowly, licking his lips and fiddling with his glasses, 'I would say she was rather acid.'

'Why?'

'She was a snotty bloody cow,' Bardolle translated into words they could all understand. 'First she didn't want to see us, then we had to stand in front of her self-important desk while she sat behind it like a headmistress preparing to cane a couple of schoolboys.'

'Thank you, Bardolle,' Pel interrupted him. 'What exactly did she say to the news of her father?'

Bardolle flipped open his notebook. 'She said, Oh dear, how terrible, I'm not surprised. My father is a stupid old fool, I expect he's wandered off somewhere and got himself mugged.' He looked up from his notes and added, 'She said it in that tone of voice too, not a hint of emotion.'

Pel turned to Pujol again. 'What do you make of it?' he asked.

Pujol pressed himself against the wall. 'Not a lot,' he whispered, 'but I'd like to meet her husband, he deserves a medal.'

'Get the car, Pujol, we're going out,' Pel announced happily. 'Bardolle, you come too. If we set off now we'll catch them filling their faces at the table and she won't be able to play headmistress with me.'

When they pulled up outside the property, Pel noticed the large painted sign over the door: 'BARON-BLAU, VIG-NOBLE DE MÂCON, Fine wines bottled by the family.' It looked good but didn't deceive the discerning for a minute. Pel stepped out into the scorching courtyard and looked around; the buildings were neat and clean, the tractors carefully parked and to one side a brand new *vendange* machine was in evidence.

'Getting ready for the grape picking,' Bardolle said. 'It's a bit early though, you don't usually see those things until the beginning of September.'

A young dog bounded up to them obviously pleased by the company, followed by a middle-aged man wiping his mouth on a stained handkerchief.

'Yeah, wha'd'you want?' he asked elegantly.

Pel showed him his identification. 'My men called here and saw Madame Lorette Baron-Blau and her manager,' he explained. 'Being their superior officer I've come back for clarification on the statements taken.' It sounded good,

good enough to impress even the acid Lorette if she happened to be listening.

The man only laughed. 'You won't catch those two here again until tomorrow morning. I'm the only mug about at this time of day. The Marocains'll be back at two if you want to talk to them.'

'And Monsieur François Baron?'

'That's me, mate.'

Showing them into the large office filled with filing cabinets and a brand new computer, he sat in the one chair behind the huge desk putting his boots on the collection of papers.

'Only chance I ever get to sit here,' he said, 'to eat me flipping lunch. Now, what can I do for you?'

'I had hoped to see your wife. However, as we're alone I'll come straight to the point: do you know Mariline Philibert?'

Baron's boots thumped on the floor and he stood wide-eyed in front of them.

'Who told you?'

'Who told us what?'

'That I knew her.'

'We worked it out.'

Baron walked round behind them and carefully closed the door. 'Look,' he said, 'it was nothing. She's a nice girl, the moment she found out I was married she refused to see me again. Has something happened to her?'

'One could say that,' Pel agreed. 'She was involved in a road accident three days ago.'

'*Merde alors!* Is she all right?'

'By the grace of God, yes, she is, but she could have been killed. Her brakes had been drained.'

Baron sat down again, rubbed his forehead then opened the drawer of the desk. Bardolle was beside him in a second. 'Don't try anything,' he boomed.

'Hey, steady on,' Baron cried, pinned to the chair by

Bardolle's massive hands. 'I was only going to offer you a drink.'

He was allowed to extract a bottle of *marc* and four small tumblers. 'I'm sorry, but I don't see the connection,' he said, pouring carefully. 'Surely you don't think I did it?'

'It is a possibility,' Pel pointed out.

'Never, not in a million years.' He handed them each a glass, draining his own in a gulp. 'Oh come on, I'm a poor bloody peasant not a prospective murderer.'

'This property doesn't look like that of a poor bloody peasant,' Pel said, 'more like a well-run business.'

'That's my wife, I just work here.'

'Tell us about it,' Pel insisted, sniffing suspiciously at his drink.

'My father died when I was nineteen and I inherited the twenty-one hectares of vineyards. I was green and fell for the offers the bank made to lend me money. I bought new tractors, pruning material and a car, I dreamt of building it up into one of the best *vignobles* in the area. But the weather was unkind, I was inexperienced and the bank was without pity; very soon I found *l'huissier* knocking at the door. They'd sent the bailiffs in and I risked losing the lot, so I placed an ad for a partner to buy out half. Lorette turned up making eyes at me and flaunting folding francs. I couldn't refuse. She was well educated, a qualified accountant, young and attractive – she also wanted to win prizes producing wine. She paid my debts and we became partners. When I proposed marriage she accepted and at first it was the good life, hard work but good. After a couple of false starts she even produced our two daughters. But I found out Lorette is an ambitious woman, everything she'd done was for her not for me. She loves money more than she ever loved me or the girls and the better we did the more she wanted. We bought up the surrounding vineyards, pestering the peasants and raising

71

the price until they gave in and sold up. Then the labourers arrived. She didn't want to work outside any more, she wanted to be a businesswoman in the office. She built the house, a grand affair five kilometres from here, and finally she employed a manager fresh out of *l'école de viticulture* and I was reduced to what I was before, a simple farmhand. A well-paid farmhand, but that's all. Our girls left home, my wife was busy stockpiling the money and I was getting bored, so I started a bit of private life myself, you know what I mean?' He shrugged. 'But Lorette didn't like it and said if I wanted to go chasing skirts I should do it away from home, away from the eyes of the neighbours, so I tried the bars in other cities. That's how I met Mariline.'

He fell silent, sloshing some more *marc* into his glass. 'Well, that's it really, nothing more sinister than a bit on the side.'

'Does your wife know about her?'

'Sort of, she knows what I'm after when I go out alone,' he said quietly, 'but don't ask her about it – she'll deny it. When she doesn't like something she convinces herself it doesn't exist. No,' he repeated, 'please don't ask her about it, it'll cause no end of trouble.'

The Baron-Blau villa was brand new, built with Spanish-style arches and shining blue shutters. It sat importantly on top of a small hill overlooking the vineyards and was surrounded by a neatly manicured garden. It smelt of wealth.

The multi-chime door bell was answered by a young man of Pujol's age but built like a rugger forward; he sported a very deep tan. He asked them to wait and marched off down the wide echoing hall.

'That's the snotty little manager,' Bardolle said as quietly as he could.

'He looks pretty big to me. Whatever you do don't belt him,' Pel ordered.

When he came back the manager reported that Madame was not available. Pel sighed. Resigned to a battle of wits, he was prepared to cheat.

'Tell Madame', he said smoothly, 'that I would be most grateful if she would make herself available. I am a chief inspector of the Police Judiciaire and am not used to being kept waiting. If Madame cannot accord me a few minutes immediately I shall be obliged to return with a number of marked police cars all with flashing blue lights for the locals to see and sirens loud enough for the inhabitants of the entire valley to hear.'

Momentarily the manager stared at him before turning on his heel and cantering off across the floor.

'I say, well played,' Pujol said in admiration.

'Thank you. Let's hope it brings the desired result.'

It did.

Lorette looked surprisingly like her adoptive sister Maxine, hard-faced and expensively dressed. She didn't have satellite dishes suspended from her ears but she did have a generous collection of gold bracelets that clanked ominously round her wrists whenever she moved.

'This is most inconvenient,' she announced. 'We said all we had to say the last time.'

'Any intrusion is inconvenient,' Pel admitted, 'but a discreet intrusion is less inconvenient than flashing lights and blasting sirens, *n'est-ce pas*?'

'You'd better sit down,' she offered ungraciously and they perched on the edge of a hard leather sofa while she sank into a chintz-covered armchair, clanking as she arranged herself comfortably.

'Your father – ' Pel started.

'My father, was, is and will always be a mean and stupid man. He has had considerable wealth which he has seen fit to share with no one, not even my poor mother,

73

God rest her soul – he sent her to an early grave. He lives off my sister, who imagines that one day, the day he dies, she will inherit his fortune. She too is stupid. I learnt a long time ago that if I wanted something done I had to do it myself, and I have. Have I said enough?'

'Your father', Pel repeated, 'has disappeared.'

'I know.'

'Do you have any idea where he might have gone, or who may have kidnapped or even murdered him?'

'I wouldn't be surprised if Maxine or her husband had finally pushed him in the lake – he deserved it.'

'So far no body has been found in the lake.'

'*Mon Dieu!* You're serious.'

'Never more so.'

'No,' she said more slowly, 'I truly don't know what could have happened to him. I haven't seen him in years and then he laughed in my face.'

'About what, madame?'

'My marriage to a peasant. He laughed at our wedding and hasn't stopped since.'

'The wealth of which you speak, that would be the family firm, I presume?'

'He used to taunt us with it when we were younger – "be nice to me or you won't inherit a penny," that sort of thing. He was a hard-working businessman when we were children, often absent and always tight-fisted. I imagine Blau Beauté is worth a small fortune by now.'

'You know about the robbery at the airport?'

'I was told,' she said, looking at Bardolle and Pujol.

'It doesn't interest you?'

'Who needs his potty perfume?' She brushed a stray lock of hair back into place, her bracelets crashing about on her arm as she moved. 'I've made enough money to buy Chanel or Dior without having to worry about the Blau stink bombs.'

It was time to change the subject. 'Your husband works

74

for you, madame, but you also employ a manager. That seems a little strange, considering it was his land to begin with.'

'You can think what you like, Chief Inspector, the fact remains that while my husband is a good worker he does not have a viticulturist's diploma. He doesn't complain and he's very well paid for what he does.'

'You have a good working relationship, then?'

'One could say that.'

'With no secrets?'

'Everyone has secrets, no doubt even you have a few.' Pel thought hard but couldn't for the life of him come up with a single one. Lorette suddenly leant forward. 'Just a minute,' she said, clanking wildly. 'What's he been telling you? Has he been showing off about his exploits with women? Silly fool, if he can't be more discreet I'll . . .' She stopped speaking, her mouth a thin line of loathing while she thought of a suitable punishment.

'I'll remove his company car.' She smiled. 'He won't get very far on what's left: a muddy tractor!'

6

That evening Pel managed twenty-four lines on the Game-boy, and his wife noticed with pleasure that he didn't smoke a cigarette for a whole hour. She was hoping to interrupt his game with a short conversation about antiques but was glad she hadn't because when Madame Routy marched in with their coffee and spoke to him he was furious.

'Good God, woman, can't you see I'm concentrating? Now I shall have to start all over again. Go back to your coven and add a bit more bat's wing to your cauldron!'

His wife put a lump of sugar in his coffee, stirred it and left it to go cold by his elbow. That night, when she at last persuaded him to retire to bed, he slipped into a restless sleep to dream of small geometric shapes piling up on top of him.

Cousin Roger was as good as his word. He'd met Pel for a drink and listened to what he wanted before spending the next hour discussing the problems of the world and the imbeciles in power. They were both members of the very exclusive Bigots' Club; Pel was founder, Cousin Roger was honorary treasurer. After that the membership list had been closed.

Since their meeting Cousin Roger had been sniffing around the accountancy world and after chatting at length with a number of colleagues came up with an interesting fact. 'Mad Max was intending to buy her place in the perfume world,' he told Pel.

Cousin Roger had never been inside a Hôtel de Police

before and was like a small child on an outing to the zoo. Dragging him down the corridor towards his office, Pel was obliged to push him forcefully in the right direction. Roger hesitated at every open door, hoping to catch a glimpse of a famous criminal or a bit of police brutality. At last, closed into Pel's office, he caused chaos on the switchboard by pressing all the buttons on the intercom to see who was at the other end.

Pel unplugged everything, replugged the telephone and called for coffee, hot and strong. The moment he'd put the phone down it rang. Snatching it up again he shouted, 'I haven't come in yet,' and slammed it back down.

Annie arrived with the steaming cups. 'The *juge d'instruction*, Maître Brisard, is not pleased,' she said, smiling. 'He says you just insulted him.'

'Sort him out, Annie, I haven't time. Now sod off, please, and let me listen to this lunatic.'

After she'd left, Cousin Roger lit a cigarette, offering the packet to Pel who fell on it as if it would save his life.

'Cor,' Roger said, 'it's all go here, isn't it?'

The office was already boiling hot, thanks to the large windows that allowed the sun outside to transform it into a furnace. Pel removed his jacket, showering cinders and ash all over his desk; it looked as if it was about to burst into flames. When the smoke had died down and he'd salvaged the singed paperwork he fell exhausted into his chair, and it was only just gone eight. Some mornings should be cancelled.

'You were saying?'

'Oh, yes.' Roger sat to attention. 'Mad Max, that's what she's called in business circles, either Mad Max or Maximum, your friend Maxine Blau, she's been trying to pull off a deal for six months now with a small but well-established perfume factory in Provence. The whisper is that she was desperate to get it then a couple of days ago she withdrew her offer completely. The perfume factory were holding out for a better offer and are now prepared to sign for less money, but she doesn't want to know.'

'Interesting,' Pel agreed. 'What about the rest of them?'

'The old boy has a private income from a block of holiday flats he has on the coast – they bring in more than enough to keep him comfortable. He pays his daughter an allowance for the privilege of living in her house; he also pays for all his food, drink, electricity and so on.

'Lorette has almost the same reputation as Mad Max, a keen businesswoman who's built an empire from a bankrupt vineyard. Jacqueline Blau, the divorcee, ricochets from one disaster to another. She has a taste for men without work and a terrific thirst for red wine. But', he added, 'no registered debts and the bailiffs in Ste Etienne haven't had dealings with her yet.'

'So there's only Mad Max who's been behaving financially irrationally.'

'I suppose you could interpret it like that,' Roger agreed.

Darcy called to say the morning meeting was in progress and after a certain amount of difficulty Pel manoeuvred Cousin Roger out into the corridor and towards the stairs. With a sigh of relief he shoved him gently into the street.

'Any time, old chap,' Roger called as he walked away. It was market day and Pel was pleased to see him rapidly swallowed up by the bustling crowd.

He wiped his fevered brow and climbed the staircase again. In this heat the Préfecture should consider installing lifts, he thought bitterly – poor bloody policemen, slogging on in this weather while everyone else was packing their suitcases and heading for the beach. All he had to look forward to was a long climb up the millions of stairs and back to the grind.

The sergeants' room was surprisingly quiet when he pushed the door open; his staff were studying their files and smiling. Pel demanded to know what was so amusing. Darcy handed him a fax. 'This just came in,' he said.

It was from the Sète police and almost made Pel smile with them, but he stopped himself just in time.

'The crafty old devil,' he said. 'I wonder what the hell he's up to.' He slammed the paper on to the table. 'So Blau fell flat on his face at Avignon station and he's been taken to hospital for observation. De Troq', get on to the mournful Commissaire Clouet, he's been helpful in the past, and find out what happened, then call the hospital. I still want to talk to the old boy.'

As de Troq' left the room, Pel turned towards Darcy. 'What's on the agenda for today?' he asked. 'And think of the heat, keep it simple.'

'I'd like to clear up the question of Mariette. Perhaps now we know it's just a nickname it may jog the priest's memory.'

'If she confessed to him, he's not going to tell us even now. She may be the key to the Blau mess, but we don't know anything yet. Your idea that Mariette's just a nickname is possible, I agree, but we haven't got precious time to waste on what could turn out to be a wild-goose chase. Anyway,' Pel added, 'now we know the old boy is alive and well we can simply ask him.'

But he was wrong.

De Troq' was worried. Having got through to the hospital where Monsieur Blau had been taken, and after waiting an eternity listening to a very bad rendering of electronic Mozart that the switchboard had automatically given him while they searched for the correct building, department, ward and at last room number, he was then able to hear the old boy himself in a state of near hysteria.

'They're trying to kill me,' he screamed down the phone. 'Get me out of here, I implore you.'

De Troq' had tried to calm him down but to no avail; the old man was convinced someone was about to slit his throat. When Pel joined him he'd persuaded Commissaire Clouet to put a guard outside Blau's door and after another long wait and a bit more Mozart the doctor responsible for his treatment came on the line. Pel turned the phone up and listened in.

'We had a job getting him through the doors of the hospital and quite a fight before he'd accept examination,' the doctor was saying, 'and he has been going downhill ever since. I've given him something to help the crisis. He was shaking with fear an hour ago, clinging to me and begging me not to let them kill him.'

'Has he told you who's after him?' de Troq' asked.

'He simply says "them". When he was first admitted he seemed fine, just an old man who was rather overexcited and cross. He'd bruised his knees when he fell but nothing more serious. Keeping him here was a formality. His daughter wanted to make absolutely sure that there would be no complications after his little adventure, and it was a good thing, we've found cardiac irregularities.'

That afternoon Maxine Blau rang from Sète and demanded to speak to Pel. She was furious – not, as he expected, because her father had run away from home and, now caught, was accusing an unknown party of trying to murder him, but about a surprise she'd found locked into a cupboard in his office. 'I was very patient,' she said angrily, 'but he's caused no end of trouble. Files have been mislaid, documents left unsigned, orders not filled – it's been impossible here. The moment my back's turned I find the factory in turmoil.'

As no one was looking Pel allowed himself a flicker of a grin. Considering her father had very little to do with the business any more, it seemed to him that the employees had found an excellent excuse to be temporarily lazy.

'I just had to take over,' she went on. 'His office took a day and a half to empty. I needed a shovel to clear just the desktop.'

'He'd only been missing a couple of days,' Pel pointed out. She'd already virtually boxed up the old boy himself and sent him off to the rubbish tip, his office had been emptied and his desk cleared. He was delighted to remember Darcy hadn't touched his belongings when he was kidnapped and thought to be done for.* He decided second-in-command detectives were kinder than daughters.

'A couple of days is a long time when you're running a firm like this one,' she snapped. 'I had to act quickly to save us from disaster. When our competitors found out about the robbery they spread rumours of financial difficulty and our retailers were losing confidence – it's been dreadful. But more dreadful was what I found in the cupboard. It was locked, you see, so I called the janitor and insisted that he break it open. There behind a lot of useless rubbish were the precious sample bottles of perfume. He never sent them!'

So they'd been right, the box that was stolen had contained something else. Pel sighed. 'So what did he send?' he asked.

'How should I know? I went straight to the hospital, but he was drugged, I couldn't get any sense out of him at all, I think he's finally gone off his rocker.'

'But he was still robbed.'

Maxine's laugh was hollow. 'But we haven't lost the perfume, thank God. It was probably one of his practical jokes. I should drop the enquiry if I were you, Chief Inspector.'

* See *Pel and the perfect partner*.

Pel pushed his glasses up on to his forehead and stared at the ceiling. 'Madame,' he said coldly, 'armed men held up a plane at the airport here and broke open the hold, they removed the contents of your father's box, they touched nothing else – that suggests to me that they at least knew what was in there and that it was extremely valuable. Or', he added desperately, 'the whole thing is one huge hoax.'

This information was obviously being digested at the other end of the phone until Maxine made a charming suggestion. 'Then you'd better find out,' she said and rang off.

Pel was in a foul mood for the rest of the day. It made no difference to his team, he usually was, but his house-keeper, who for once was innocently making an apple tart in the kitchen, caught the brunt of it when he arrived home. He sacked her the moment he stepped through the door and again before heading up the stairs to take a cooling shower. The weather was impossible; he was still hot standing dripping on to the bathroom carpet. He wiped the mirror clear and took a look at himself. Escaping that nightmare, he hurried into the bedroom to cover the horror with clean clothes. Now, he promised himself, a good long drink and an equally good long go with the Gameboy.

Settling himself comfortably into an armchair, he thought again about what his young neighbour had said about the computer game being like police work; a logical puzzle which required the player to juggle odd-shaped pieces to fit them into the right places. The Blau robbery had one piece missing: the knowledge of what was in the blasted crate. The Philibert case had a piece missing: knowing why someone would want to annihilate a poor inoffensive and rather pretty student. Lorette didn't like her husband's indiscretions but put up with them if the neighbours weren't aware of his clandestine cavortings.

François, her husband, thought Mariline was a charming young woman; he wasn't thwarted in love, all he'd ever done was shake her hand. It didn't add up.

He very nearly brained Madame Routy who, having put the apple tart in the oven, was now laying the table for supper. Pel was convinced she deliberately made as much noise as possible as she marched in and out, stamping across the *carrelage* floor, to chuck porcelain and silver about just behind his ear. The Gameboy winked at him and made its infuriating rude noise to let him know he'd lost. That was it. Although it was suffocating outside, life inside was utterly impossible. He heaved himself from the chair and made for the garden. Perhaps Yves was lurking in the vicinity with a spare beer. As he stepped off the shaded terrace, he felt the weight of the evening heat on his shoulders. The weather had to break soon. Looking up at the cloudless sky, he felt a storm brewing. But the thunder and lightning didn't come, not until the next morning.

7

The thunder was no more than a small article in the papers. They'd got the story of the Blau perfume being found at the factory; millions of readers all over France had been told that the police were baffled. 'What, then,' the journalists asked, 'was stolen from the plane?' Although Pel had to admit that their information was correct and that they hadn't exaggerated, he was furious. Where the hell had they got the story from? He'd long suspected Misset of slipping the odd snippet to the press for a bit of pocket money but had never been able to prove anything.

Pel charged into the sergeants' room. 'Misset!' he roared. 'What's this?'

Pulling himself from a slouch to a sitting position, the sergeant shuffled to attention. 'A newspaper, Patron,' he replied, his brow furrowed with uncertainty.

Pel pointed at the article. 'This, you fool,' he shouted.

'An article about the airport robbery, I was just reading it.'

Misset's life was saved by Nosjean coming through the door at a rate of knots and almost rushing straight up his boss's back. He screeched to a halt, but Pujol, who was close on his heels and moving far too fast for a junior, didn't manage the emergency stop as well; he catapulted into Nosjean, who collided finally with Pel. The tangle took a minute to sort out. Pel, who'd been teetering dangerously on one leg, managed to regain his balance and spun round, ready to kill whoever it was with as many insults as he could muster, but Nosjean got in first.

'Patron,' he gasped, brushing himself off, 'Pujol's come up with something.'

'Whatever it is, it'll wait,' Pel bellowed. 'You should both be issued with speeding tickets, your behaviour is totally irresponsible.'

'Sorry, Patron, but I didn't expect to find you parked in the doorway.'

'Enough!' Pel held up his hand and marched from the office. Misset breathed a sigh of relief and slid back into his slouch.

Aware that he was being followed, Pel crashed back into his own room and snatched up the packet of cigarettes so Nosjean couldn't help himself. Since he'd started smoking again he'd picked up Darcy's habit of whipping everyone else's weeds on the pretext that he could honestly say to his wife he hadn't bought any.

Savagely placing a Gauloise in his mouth, Pel scowled at them. 'Have you seen the papers?' he demanded.

'Patron, Pujol's been doing his homework again. He came up with something that may be important.'

'Well, don't just stand there, tell me.' Pel took a cigarette from the packet in his hand and placed it beside the first between his lips. Realising his error, he ripped them both from his mouth, crushed them to dust over the overflowing wastepaper basket and took a third, throwing the now half-empty packet on the desk in disgust. Nosjean calmly helped himself.

'In the report on the interview at Beauzile', Pujol whispered, 'it was noted that a young woman was asking about the inhabitants of the village during the war. The priest said she'd introduced herself as Lillie, a student researching the modern history of Burgundy.'

'Speak up, I can hardly hear you.'

'Yes, sir,' Pujol yelled.

'There's no need to shout, I'm not deaf.'

'No, sir.'

'Get on with it, man.'

'Mariline Philibert is a student of history here in the city,' Pujol announced.

'So?'

'Lillie, sir, that's what she's called by her friends. I did a bit of asking around, sir.'

'Pujol! Whatever I've said about you in the past, I take it all back, but stop calling me sir!'

'Yes, sir, Patron, Pel.'

Pel sighed but decided he was too valuable to be fired. 'Pujol, find Mariline, Lillie Philibert and ask her the obvious. Nosjean, you'd better accompany him in case he goes into shock.'

After they'd disappeared it occurred to Pel that Mariline was in the wrong file. She'd started off as a victim of a provoked traffic accident, now she'd crossed the desk to become part of the Blau investigation. Could the two be connected?

He had to talk to the old boy Blau but after fighting with the hospital personnel and their recording of Mozart for a good five minutes the ward sister refused to put him through, saying he was resting and could not be disturbed. He decided to risk speaking to Maxine but she wasn't in the office. At last he located her in the lakeside château.

'He's due out tomorrow and I have a lot of organising to do here at home,' she explained. 'A full-time nurse will be arriving at the end of the week but for the moment I shall have to care for him myself.'

'He's no longer terrified of being murdered?' Pel asked.

'No,' she said quietly, 'and at last we know why he was so irrational. You see, he lived in his own apartment here and until now has always been allowed to be independent. He even did his own shopping by phone. That was the trouble – he ordered, it was delivered and he paid by cheque at the end of every month. He heated up his own food and the *femme de ménage* who comes in the morning washed up and kept him clean. I didn't think to check what he was ordering from the local supermarket or what was going out to the dustbin.' She sighed deeply. 'It was my fault, I suppose, but it just didn't occur to me. He'd pour himself an aperitif at lunchtime, a few minutes later he'd forget and pour himself another and so it went on. That's why he slept so well in the afternoon and also why he fell over occasionally – he was drunk. When he woke, it would start all over again until he went to bed. My father was an alcoholic, Monsieur Pel, and when he was admitted to hospital for observation he started suffering from withdrawal symptoms. He's cured now,' she added sadly, 'but miserable, old and waiting to die. Sometimes I wonder if he was better off before. My husband says I ought to let him drink again, keep the old blighter happy, but I can't, I'm so ashamed, he had bottles hidden all over the flat, even behind the books.'

Pel presented his condolences for her predicament and went on to ask her if he could visit her father the following day, but she hesitated.

'I don't think you should,' she said, 'not for the moment. He's aged enormously since his little exploit, plus the fact that we now know the old fool has a weak heart – he can't even smoke my husband's cigars any more. Couldn't it wait?'

'All I want to know is what he put in the box he sent to Burgundy. It is essential – perhaps you'd ask him and ring me back with the answer.'

Surprisingly she agreed.

Late that afternoon Nosjean and Pujol came back into his office after seeing Mariline Philibert.

'Pujol was right,' Nosjean said triumphantly, 'she's the Lillie who went to see the priest at Beauzile. She'd been

87

doing a project on the Second World War and instead of researching the battles or the Resistance like the rest of her class, she decided to follow the lives of the refugees. She's been all over the place hunting down the men and women who survived and stayed in France. Beauzile was just one of the stories she was following up. She also saw the owner of the château there and finally went to see the curé to try and find out what happened to the Pole, Nowak or Blau, but with no luck. However, when the report of the airport robbery appeared in the papers it named Blau Beauté as the owners of the box, so she set off for Sète to see the old boy. Half an hour later they were cutting her out of the wreck of her car.'

'So she's never seen him?'

'Nope, and it doesn't look very likely that she will. She's got no money for train fares and now she's got no car. She's tried writing but obviously has received no reply.'

'If she's so poor, how does she run a car?'

'It was an old banger, Patron, a Peugeot 505. The fact that it was good and solid probably saved her life, but it was ancient and only insured third party. Her father paid for it and the insurance as a present for getting into university, but the petrol she pays for herself, she'd just filled it up.'

'Does she know anything about the Blau family we don't?'

'That, unfortunately, I can't say. Her unfinished files were with her tutor when we spoke to her.'

It was food for thought: perhaps it wasn't an ex-boyfriend or a maniac that had drained the brake fluid from her car, perhaps it was something she'd turned up on the Blau family. Pel wanted her notes.

'I doubt that she'll simply hand over months of hard work, Patron,' Nosjean pointed out.

'Take her out for a slap-up meal, the poor kid seems

permanently hungry,' Pel suggested generously, 'while Pujol makes photocopies.'

The following day, while Pel was still waiting for Maxine Blau's telephone call, Nosjean and Pujol set off towards the university again to find Mariline and her precious notes. They finally tracked her down and carefully negotiated her acceptance of handing over the file for copying while she was treated to lunch in a decent restaurant. She was reticent but gave in when the smell of *boeuf bourgignon* wafted encouragingly through to the bar from the kitchens. Pujol disappeared at the speed of light with her notes grasped tightly in his hands while Nosjean escorted Lillie through to the dining-room.

Pel was grumpily toying with a plate of cold meat and even colder salad at his desk; he didn't want to leave it in case lightning struck. It did. As four o'clock chimed outside his window the telephone trilled and snatching it up he heard Maxine's highly excited voice.

'He's done it again,' she cried, 'he's disappeared into thin air, and in his condition too.'

Monsieur Blau hadn't been at the hospital when she'd arrived to take him home. The hospital staff were scratching their heads and wondering what all the fuss was about – they'd already discharged him into the capable hands of his daughter and, they pointed out, because of the trouble they'd had with this particular patient's family they had asked for proof of identification from the daughter and had been satisfied with what they'd seen. Furthermore, Monsieur Blau had reassured them himself that the woman concerned was who she said she was.

'It was my damn sister,' Maxine told Pel, 'Jacqueline. God knows what she was doing down here interfering. She hasn't been to see my father for years and that was only with her hand out asking for money.'

Pel called the police at Ste Etienne and within an hour had confirmation that Jacqueline was not at her residence. Her companion, Monsieur Willis, had told them she'd gone to Avignon to see her father who was in hospital there. It all sounded logical and perfectly normal, except that now they'd both disappeared.

The hospital reiterated what Maxine had said and he had to accept that it was highly probable that the two missing Blaus would turn up very soon with a full explanation of where they'd been. It was likely that the old man just wanted to be driven nice and slowly home after being cooped up for over a week under the strict attention of the medical team.

Nosjean and Pujol came in a little later, pleased with themselves: Pujol because he'd managed to photocopy the entire one hundred and fifteen pages of Mariline's research, and Nosjean because he'd had a jolly good lunch at the expense of the police force with a very pretty and intelligent young woman – he just hoped no one would tell Mijo.

Their smiles dissolved, however, when Pel thrust the document back at them and told them to get reading.

'Underline anything that may be significant,' he shouted as they left his office.

During the morning meeting the next day, Pujol informed them of what they'd learnt. 'For the most part it's a sad story of an educated Pole who found himself in France tending the vegetable garden and the pigs at the château at Beauzile,' he said. 'The Germans changed his name but left him fairly well alone. But, when defeat became inevitable and they were preparing to leave, gathering up anything of value to take with them, they had him in for questioning again. Then he disappeared.'

'It seems to be his party trick,' Pel said glumly.

90

'There were rumours', Pujol went on, 'that he'd been beaten to death in custody but months later news was received saying how he'd run away and hidden, terrified they might decide to take him with them or worse.'

'Who received this news?'

'The vicomte at the château. He's dead now, but the son told Mariline that that year there was a Christmas party, the whole village was invited to celebrate, er. . .' He looked quickly at the file. '. . . normality and liberation, and it was there that the news was announced. The vicomte's son was only a child then but old enough to remember the cheers of the villagers when they knew Nowak-Blau was safe. The Pole had been liked because he was a modest man and worked hard without complaining. Then there's a gap in Mariline's notes until the newspaper report of the airport hold-up, which she cut out and added to the file. She's underlined Blau Beauté of Sète, the owners of the crate, and written in the margin is the phone number of his apartment and the date she crashed her car – she was on her way to meet him in person.'

'So that means either someone in the city is simply having fun causing death and destruction on the motorway or someone didn't want Mariline identifying Blau as the Polish refugee,' Pel concluded.

It was decided to let this information stay in the Blau file. As Debray pointed out, causing road accidents was rather out of date; if there was a nutter wanting to kill or maim, he'd more likely use a bomb, it was the fashionable murder weapon. Pel agreed. They were already well and truly involved in the airport hold-up and the mystery about what was stolen; now it seemed possible that Mariline had inadvertently crossed paths with a bandit.

That afternoon the storm really broke. Electricity flickered overhead between the rapidly advancing clouds, then the hot wind tore into the city, whipping rubbish up and swirling it through the streets. Anyone outside pulled their thin summer clothes round them, bent their heads and ran for cover. As the skies turned black, lights were switched on in offices and shops, and the angry thunder that had been hurtling about the heavens cracked into forked lightning. The rain came almost immediately, falling in huge drops on to the scorched earth, creating small explosions in the remaining dust, turning into deep puddles within minutes as the hard ground refused to absorb it.

Pel stood at his window and watched the gloom settle over his beautiful Burgundy. He saw Nosjean struggling back from an unpleasant lunch with his wife. He didn't look happy at all; Pel would have to have a word and cheer him up. He winced as the weather waged its war overhead, and Nosjean wondered which obliging busybody had told Mijo about his lunch with Mariline.

At five thirty, while the storm was subsiding, the other members of Pel's team began arriving at the Hôtel de Police looking as if they'd been for a swim fully clothed in a whirlpool. In the sergeants' room reports were typed up as the men dripped merrily on to the floor and just as their thoughts turned to going home another form of lightning struck.

As they gathered their raincoats and prepared to leave, the phone rang in Pel's office. Seconds later he burst in. 'That's it,' he bellowed. 'No one goes home yet.'

The grumbling started as Nosjean reached for a cigarette and dragged at it with the same devotion as his boss. He had a feeling that telling Mijo he was working late wouldn't help the happy home.

Pel watched him exhale. 'Still smoking, I see,' he said cheerfully.

'Yes, Patron,' came the miserable reply.

'Good man, keep it up, we're going to need all the help we can get – the old boy Blau is dead.'

8

Commissaire Clouet of Avignon was still waiting patiently as Darcy followed Pel back to his office to listen to the report of Blau's death.

'I was called out to a death at the Hôtel Majestic in the centre of town, nothing odd, just a formality,' he told them, 'an old man who'd passed away in his sleep. His daughter was fairly hysterical but we got her calmed down enough for her to tell us that the dead man had a dicky heart. The doctor had pronounced him dead and was making arrangements for the body to be removed for autopsy when hysteria broke out again.' He sighed sadly. 'So I did the explaining. His last twenty-four hours hadn't been spent in a hospital therefore an autopsy had to be carried out – law, I said, but you know what women are, she started sobbing all over the place again. Anyway, it was all cleared up and off went the body. Then half an hour ago, just as I was signing my report on the affair, Madame Maxine Blau telephones and gives me such an earful I almost arrested her on the spot. She told me in no uncertain terms that I must, repeat must, get in touch with you and tell you her father was dead. *Et voilà*,' he ended, sounding more melancholic than ever, 'mission accomplished.'

Pel thanked him for his recitation and asked to be informed of the results of the autopsy as soon as Clouet had them. The Commissaire agreed in a voice that suggested he was about to attend his own funeral. Darcy thought Pel was a difficult little bugger at times but he was far less depressing than Clouet; he'd never realised how lucky he was to have such a cheerful boss.

93

'What are you grinning for?' Pel yelled at him. 'Get Mad Max on the phone.'

'Now we'll never know what was in the bloody box . . .' Pel stormed round his office waiting for the call to come through. When it finally did, he wished it hadn't – she was full of accusations about lack of protection for her father and demanding to know why he'd been released to her stupid sister.

Pel, of course, pointed out that while the old man was screaming that someone was trying to murder him they had made sure that a policeman was outside his door at all times, but once the alcoholism had been diagnosed and he'd calmed down, there had been no reason to continue. The fact that he'd left with the wrong daughter was hardly his fault nor the hospital's. In his opinion they had been very prudent in asking for proof of identification from Jacqueline before allowing them to leave.

'What time did you arrive, madame?'

'At two o'clock, as instructed by the nurses,' she said crossly emphasising that at least she'd been efficient.

'And obviously you didn't see your father or your sister even briefly, in the car-park for instance.'

'Of course not, you silly little man, if I had I'd have stopped them. You can recognise her van anywhere. Fancy going to collect an ailing elderly man in an old jalopy with Ban the Bomb stickers all over it that stinks of her revolting goats.'

There had been a sharp intake of breath. Pel wasn't amused at being called a silly little man.

'And I'm told they're going to do an autopsy,' she shrieked on. 'What on earth for, I can't imagine. He was suffering from a weak heart as well as being weak in the head. I would have thought it was obvious – the specialist didn't treat it properly and the drugs he prescribed weren't efficacious. That hospital has a lot to answer for.'

'Madame,' Pel asked cautiously, 'your father, Monsieur Josephe Blau, did he have Polish origins?'

'What's that got to do with it?'

'I'm not sure,' Pel admitted, 'but I'd like to know.'

'So what if my father wasn't born in France? He's always paid French taxes and has created a lot of employment for the locals. Ridiculous question!'

'So your father is Polish by birth?' Pel insisted.

'Good God, man, what the hell does it matter? Anyway,' she added with a sniff, 'he's dead now.'

As Pel put the phone down his ears were still ringing. He tried to talk to the doctor in charge and the admissions nurse but of course everyone had gone home; only the night staff remained and they knew nothing.

When he at last arrived home, he found his wife sitting listening to *La Traviata*. On the table was a small silver tray with a glass of his favourite whisky, a brand new packet of Gauloises and the Gameboy. He picked up the collection and, kissing her on the cheek, settled himself for the evening.

Darcy found Kate listening to Dire Straits, dancing as she sorted and folded the mounds of dry washing on their vast kitchen table. He kissed her passionately and helped himself to a glass of wine while watching her work. She was smiling and beautiful, more lovely than usual, glowing with health and happiness. Then he noticed the tiny clothes she was sorting. He took another long sip at his drink, trying to work it out, the smile on his face broadening into a grin.

'Does that mean . . .' he started.

'It does.' She grinned back. 'I'll be putting on weight for a while.'

Darcy headed for the cellar to find the bottle of Bollinger he'd been hiding.

Nosjean wearily put his key in the door. As he pushed it open he found the apartment was in darkness. A few pin-pricks of light pierced the thin curtains at the windows: it wasn't a power cut, or the park wouldn't be lit. He crept into the kitchen and flicked the switch up, allowing the neon to flicker then glow. On the formica table was a note: 'Very tired, please don't disturb me. If Erica wakes up the bottle's in the fridge, it's your turn to feed the baby.' He sighed heavily, poured himself a large brandy and went out to the cool balcony to enjoy a couple of dozen cigarettes. He'd given in and bought a packet on the way home.

When Clouet rang the following day to give Pel the results of the autopsy, no one was surprised to be told Monsieur Blau had died of a heart attack and Pel was forced to agree that they should at last allow the hotel staff into the sealed room to clean it and change the sheets. That seemed to be that, except that Mad Max was still screaming at anyone she could find and demanding the release of the body for burial. Pel asked Clouet if he could delay it until after lunch.

'I expect she'll get me sacked for inefficiency,' he replied dolefully, 'that woman has a lot of clout, but as it's you, Pel, I suppose you have your reasons. I'll see what I can do.'

Pel spoke to the hospital and discovered a number of facts, one of which was the vehicle Blau left the hospital in. He was surprised by this piece of information; usually when asking a witness about a car, he was told it had four wheels and a couple of doors, even the colour escaped most people. However, the girl was adamant. 'He was a nice old boy,' she said, 'his daughter wasn't, she was a pushy sort, you know, that's why I decided to do my stuff and ask for her *carte d'identité*. She didn't like that but she showed me, couldn't wait to be off, almost dragging poor Monsieur Blau through the door. Well, I watched them as they went out and funnily enough they've got the same car as us, a big white Nevada brake, we only bought ours a couple of weeks ago for the kids and their bikes, cost us a fortune and it was second-hand, it's only because I work as well as my husband that we could afford it.'

Although the girl seemed to be suffering from verbal diarrhoea, Pel had listened and was interested to note the exact description of the car and the fact that Jacqueline had been in a hurry. Probably didn't want to cross paths with Mad Max – who would?

'Tell me,' he asked, 'was Monsieur Blau in possession of the medication he needed for his heart?'

'Oh, that I don't know, you'll have to ask the nurse who was on duty. Do you want me to put you through?'

It was a pleasure doing business with someone so bright and helpful. Pel found the nurse less forthcoming but her memory was working. She confirmed that she'd carefully given her patient his pills and also carefully explained how many he had to take a day. 'I didn't bother to tell his daughter because she already knew. She'd been ringing up the whole time wanting to know what was happening, she was a nuisance, the doctor refused her calls in the end, and anyway,' she added, 'the instructions were clearly marked on the prescription attached to the drugs. All Madame had to do was read it, then she'd know we were telling the truth.'

With the name of the drug written carefully on his notepad – it'd taken three attempts to get the spelling right – Pel telephoned Dr Cham, head of the Pathology Department. However, it was Dr Boudet, a massive and jovial general practitioner, who answered. He enjoyed turning Pel green with the details of blood and guts, and to his delight had been appointed as one of the official police doctors which meant he could spend his spare time

97

helping Cham with the dead bodies that passed through the autopsy lab daily. Their sense of humour was sick but their science was sharp, and although Pel always needed something strong to settle his stomach after any communication with them, he never regretted the information they gave him. They were a macabre cabaret.

'Hello, Pel,' Boudet boomed cheerfully. 'Got a nice smelly *cadavre* for us to play with?'

'Not yet,' Pel replied, swallowing hard at the thought of what they might be up to, 'but I do have a question.'

'Fire away, we're all ears. I've turned you up so Cham can hear as well – he's a bit busy at the moment, can't get the chain-saw started, up to his ears in bloody motor oil.'

His delicate choice of words started Pel's stomach churning. 'Acebutolol,' he said with difficulty, 'tell me about it.'

'Everything or just the basics?'

'Keep it basic, I'm only a poor humble detective. I can hardly say the word, so stay simple and I might understand.'

'Acebutolol', Boudet rolled the word round his mouth, 'is a drug used for heart patients, keep the old muscle working properly, but it's dangerous. If its absorption is interrupted the patient'll end up here pretty fast.'

'Go on,' Pel encouraged.

'If you stop taking it suddenly, it'll provoke a heart attack.'

'Fatal?'

'Heart attacks often are.'

Pel heard the faint buzzing of a small chain-saw at work and reached hurriedly for his cigarette, thanked Boudet and rang off immediately. Boudet had been serious about what Cham had been up to – what on earth would a couple of pathologists be doing with a chain-saw? His mind boggled and going in search of a large glass of water he forbade himself to think about it.

Clouet was back on the phone that afternoon begging Pel for permission to release the body of Monsieur Blau. Maxine had arrived personally in Avignon and was creating merry hell.

When Pel announced he was going to ask for a second autopsy Clouet sounded as if he was ready to shoot himself.

'*Courage,*' Pel said, glad that Blau hadn't died in his own blessed Burgundy. 'If she really gets out of control, tell her to ring me.' Pel was surprisingly brave on the end of a phone.

'I'll do that,' Clouet said. 'Just one more thing, Pel. Before I let the cleaners into the room where he died I did a bit of ferreting about myself. The only thing I found which may be of interest was a box of pills with an unpronounceable name.'

'Acebutolol?' Pel asked, reading it from his notes.

'That's the stuff. They were under the bed.'

Pel didn't feel very brave when he discovered that his favourite pretty female *juge d'instruction* was on holiday, which meant that the pompous ass, Brisard, would be in charge. However, it had to be done, so picking up his files he wearily waded his way through the weather to his office.

The storms were over and although there was a new freshness to the air, making it breathable, the sun was shining in all its glory, sucking any lingering moisture out of the ground. It was exhaustingly hot again.

Pel struggled down the stairs, along the corridors of officialdom, in and out of doors, up another staggering flight of stairs and finally came to a halt outside Brisard's self-important door. He knocked and entered without waiting for a reply to catch the wide-hipped *juge* talking

99

softly into the phone. The caller was dispensed with quickly and, leaning his elbows on the desk, hands closing together as if he were about to say his prayers, he nodded at Pel to sit.

'I'm tempted to say I haven't come in yet,' Brisard started. 'That's what you shouted at me the last time I tried to talk to you. One doesn't appreciate that sort of reception from a senior officer of the Police Judiciaire.'

Ignoring him, Pel picked up the photograph of Brisard's wife and children. 'Good-looking family,' he lied.

'Indeed, most proud of them, my children are doing extremely well at school,' Brisard announced importantly. 'I expect my son to follow my example and go into law.'

Pel replaced the frame on the desk. 'I hope he doesn't follow your example of how to be a loving husband.' Brisard had a long-established relationship with a police-man's widow which had delighted Pel when he'd found out. Brisard didn't know how much he knew, but the moment the subject was mentioned the wind went out of his sails and he was a little more easily manipulated.

Brisard coughed, withdrew a handkerchief from his pocket and wiped his perspiring forehead.

'You, I suppose, are the model husband?' he asked nastily.

Pel shrugged. 'I have to be, no one else would have me.'

It had always amazed Brisard that a chap like Pel, with hair that looked like strands of seaweed strewn across a rock at low tide, a dress sense that would make a tramp blush and a way of expressing himself verbally that was totally intolerable, had caught, and kept, the wealthy and intelligent woman who was now his wife. He had to admit that she was also more than acceptably attractive, but he wasn't going to flatter Pel by telling him. 'No, they wouldn't,' he agreed.

After half an hour's haggling Pel left his office with the

signed authorisation for the second autopsy to be carried out by Doc Cham. He was well satisfied. The moment he arrived back at his own desk he reached for the phone and informed the long-suffering Clouet in Avignon.

'Oh, thank God you've rung,' he cried. 'You can explain it to Madame, she's in my office at this moment.'

Mad Max was more than usually mad. 'How dare you interfere like this? You'll pay for it, you know – I know people in high places. You'll be out on your ear before you can – '

With one word Pel stopped her tirade. 'Murder,' he said clearly.

'I beg your pardon?'

'I'll pardon you, madame,' he said smugly, 'if you stop shouting your mouth off and accept that your father may have been murdered.'

There was a deathly hush at the other end of the line before a new explosion was launched into Pel's ear. 'But who?' Maxine demanded. 'Who would want to kill an innocent old man like my father? It's utterly ridiculous.'

Pel gently cut the communication and dialled the Hôtel Majestic where he asked to speak to the manager, but he couldn't be found. A few minutes later, however, he called back, apologising for his absence. 'I was on my way up to check that Monsieur Blau's room was cleared and cleaned properly. Commissaire Clouet asked me to be present but we've waited so long to do it, I don't suppose another half-hour will make any difference.'

Pel asked him about the death and waited eagerly for the reply.

'Madame Blau, Jacqueline, came down to reception at about two thirty in a fluster,' he heard. 'She'd already enquired earlier if her father had ordered breakfast then later if he'd asked for lunch to be sent up. But this time she was in a panic. The door had been locked from the inside and she couldn't get in – she was worried. I took

101

the master key and went up in the lift with her. She entered the room first and I followed, just in case. And a good thing too. Poor old chap – but he looked very peaceful. Madame was in a terrible state, needed a lot of calming down.'

'The Blau sisters have a tendency towards hysteria,' Pel agreed.

It was an ordinary story that sounded very unsuspicious – except, Pel kept asking himself, what was Jacqueline doing staying at a hotel in the centre of Avignon with a sick old man?

9

Jacqueline was back in Ste Etienne, or to be precise on the outskirts, in a scruffy rundown farmhouse with a herd of goats nibbling at the sparse greenery in the surrounding fields. As Pel and Cheriff drew up outside the house in the dusty yard, a flurry of chickens flapped inelegantly off to roost in a solitary tree. There was a tangle of brambles at one end of the yard, a couple of rickety sheds that were held together with string and wire, and just in front of them a rusting van with Ban the Bomb stickers all over it looking as if it should be abandoned permanently. Rock music was coming loudly from one of the open windows.

She would have been an attractive woman but for her ravaged appearance. Jacqueline was considerably younger than Maxine and Lorette and she definitely didn't buy her clothes from the same shop. Her T-shirt was stained, her shorts were sawn-off jeans and on the end of two long thin legs were a pair of high-heeled mules; without them she would have been about the same height as Pel. There were broken veins in her cheeks and she appeared not to have slept in weeks; her long black hair hung limply round her face like a couple of greasy curtains.

They presented their credentials and were sulkily invited into the chaos of the house. Five dogs were kicked out and the music was turned down as they sat in the scruffy kitchen. The table was covered with dirty plates while a collection of unwashed pans overflowed from the sink.

'Yeah?' she said. 'What do you want?' She grabbed a

103

cloudy glass and sloshed red wine into it from a plastic bottle. 'Want some?' she offered.

'Thank you, no,' Pel said politely. 'We've come to talk to you about your father.'

'Dead, isn't he?'

'That much we know. We are more interested in the circumstances surrounding his death.'

'Okay, I'll tell you.' She drained the glass to the bottom and filled it up again. 'Max rang me to tell me that he was in hospital, can't remember when. So what? I thought, don't know why she bothered, but you know, dad was old and I decided to visit him.'

'How did you get there?'

'Ex-husband's car. He's a prize bastard, but loaded, thought he'd do that for me to see my dying dad, and I was right. So off I jolly well went.'

'Why did you decide to go all that way? He wasn't dying at the time.'

She hesitated a moment before answering 'If you must know, I reckoned he might give me some money. Things are a bit tight at the moment, I don't know, it was worth a try. Anyway, there I was at the hospital holding his hand when he starts on about me taking him home. Why not? I said to myself, that way he'd pay for the petrol, so I bundled him into the car.'

'Was he in a hurry to get home?'

'Not in a hurry really, no, in fact he dawdled the whole time, real pain. Once we were in the car – '

'Were you present when he was given instructions about his treatment?'

'What treatment? Don't know anything about that – Oh, hang on, yes, he was carrying a little bag of goodies, they could've been his pills. As I was saying, once we were in the car, he went all funny on me and wanted to drive north and he'd tell me when to stop. Well, I wasn't going to do that, for shit's sake – I mean, Max would've killed me. I'd already whipped dad from under her nose, she was the one who was supposed to fetch him from hospital you know. The bitch who discharged him didn't want to let him out with me. Still, we sorted that one out. I told him, no way, but blimey he was stubborn, had me driving round and round in circles in the end. Well, I said we'd stop for a drink, you know, *manière*, calm us both down a bit – you're joking, he was even worse!'

'Where did you stop for a drink?'

'*Putain, j'sais pas moi*, you do ask weird questions. I don't know, haven't a clue, somewhere just off the bypass. Anyway, I hit a compromise, said I'd stay with him in Avignon for the night. Thought I'd better let Max know what the hell was going on. I got him into the Majestic but couldn't get hold of her, so I left a message on the answering machine. Rang my boyfriend and told him where I was and went back to see dad in his room. He was bribing me now, saying if I drove him north he'd buy me a new car, a house, a plane, sodding well anything I wanted. Well, it was tempting, I must say. Damn it, I thought, I'll sleep on it and work it out in the morning. I tucked him in all cosy and went down to order a light meal on a tray and after I'd finished in the dining-room I took it up.' She stopped to drain her glass again. 'Thirsty work, this story-telling, sure you don't want a drop?'

The policemen declined but she filled up again before continuing. 'Next morning, I went in to see him and he was sleeping peacefully, so I took the tray down and left him to rest, then I buggered off for breakfast. Went into town after that to buy him a newspaper and a couple of magazines, got back about midday and the bloke at reception said he hadn't rung down for breakfast or lunch. Thought he must be knackered after the hospital and so on, so I went and had a steak. While I was eating I got to thinking and all of a sudden I was in a panic. His bloody door was locked so I couldn't even get in, had to get the manager to open it, and when we did, well, there he was. Dead as a dodo. And the old sod hadn't handed over a centime. I've got myself landed with an enormous bill for the restaurant, luckily they didn't insist on payment for the room. Actually they were pretty decent, said I could take my time to recover from the shock and pay later. Maybe they'll forget.' She took a deep gulp from her glass. 'It *was* a shock too, I've never seen anyone dead before.'

Pel sat silently in the car as Cheriff drove back to the city. All the pieces fit, he said to himself, so why is it giving me indigestion?

He called Maxine to check on the message Jacqueline said she had left on her answering machine.

'I never heard it,' Maxine told him. 'My husband had invited some business colleagues to join us for the evening, and after they'd left he was the one who went to see if there'd been any calls. Jacqueline, he said, was with my father and she'd ring back the following day. Everything was fine and I wasn't to worry. But of course I did, I still didn't know where they were and I wouldn't trust that little cow with anything let alone my own father.'

'Could you tell me the name of the medication your father was taking?' There was still an idea lurking in Pel's brain and he had to clear it up.

'I spoke to the hospital regularly but after the first few days the doctor was always unavailable and, I might add, the nurses were most uncooperative.'

'But did you know the name of the drug he was taking?' Pel insisted.

'It changed almost every day until the end of his stay, the names slip my mind.'

'I believe you were a nurse once,' Pel pointed out.

'I was, but it was a long time ago and new drugs are coming on to the market every day.'

Lorette hadn't been able to hazard a guess at the name

106

either. None of the three sisters knew what their father had been taking, which was odd considering the number of times the hospital staff had been pestered for information.

At last Doc Cham arrived with the second autopsy report. It had taken time to transport Blau's body to Burgundy, do the autopsy and finally write it up. After all the impatient waiting he didn't look very encouraging as he folded his long limbs round the chair on the other side of Pel's desk and started flicking through the pages.

'There's not a lot here that'll help,' he said. 'We made the same findings as the pathologist in Avignon. Apart from his heart, he was in good health. You asked us to look for evidence of the *bétabloquant*, acebutolol, *n'est ce pas?*'

Pel nodded.

'No trace at all, which means either it wasn't prescribed, or he stopped taking it the day before.'

'The day he left the hospital.'

'You're sure you got the name right?'

'It took me three attempts to get it down on paper,' Pel replied, shuffling the contents of his desktop round until he found the relevant note. 'Look,' he said, holding it up for Cham to read for himself. 'And', he added, 'the box of albece ... lol pills was found by a policeman under his death-bed.'

'Unfortunate,' Cham admitted. 'They would have administered the drug first thing in the morning, while he was still at hospital – you know how they like to wake you up to swallow pills. He must have forgotten the lunchtime one, perhaps in the excitement of leaving, and can't have taken any that evening either, hence the *infarctus.*'

'You're in fact saying that it was accidental death?'

107

'What was his memory like? Is it possible he was tired, fell asleep before expected and was snoring happily when he should have been taking the evening dose?'

'Or could it have been removed deliberately and Blau locked in his room, which would make it murder?'

Cham closed the file. 'But you said the pills were found under the death-bed,' he said, standing up, 'and if I remember correctly from the police report I read, the door was locked from the inside.'

All the leads were heading for the same place, a dead end. Pel turned the pages in the thickening file and stopped at the description of the car Jacqueline was driving about Avignon in. It was worth a try, and anything was better than sitting cooking slowly in the heat at the Hôtel de Police.

With Didier Darras at the wheel he set off to the south-east of the city to see Jacqueline's ex-husband.

Because of the August heatwave they drove with their windows down breathing more easily as the buildings subsided and turned into empty countryside. The ex-husband was a carpenter and lived miles away from anywhere. Pel was just beginning to enjoy the scenery when Darras pulled up in front of a house; as the engine died they heard someone swearing loudly.

'Bordel de merde, où est ce putain de loup?'

'Wolf?' Pel repeated, alarmed. 'You go first, Didier – make sure the coast is clear.'

Darras approached a workshop with caution but a few seconds later came back out with a man as large as a bear. He was covered in wood shavings and laughing. 'The wolf', he was explaining, 'is one of the tools of my trade. It fits into a machine and makes life much easier when I'm doing a kilometre of *corniche* round the top of a bookcase.'

Pel still wasn't convinced. 'A kilometre of bookcase?' he asked.

'Well, it's a very large bookcase, large enough for a thousand books.' He grinned. He was built like Bardolle, the Hôtel de Police's very own Hulk, but his voice was less like a foghorn than Bardolle's, by a fraction of a decibel.

'I also have sheep,' he boomed on, opening the car door for Pel. 'The opposite shape of the wolf, the sheep fits in the wolf's mouth, but it's still for cutting wood.'

'Very interesting,' Pel said, still confused but consenting to get out of the car in the knowledge that he wasn't about to be eaten.

The carpenter, Philippe Bernard, shook his head, showering wooden confetti on to the dusty ground. 'It's sweltering out here. Come into the house where it's cooler, we'll have a glass of water – it's a good vintage this year.'

Inside, the flagstone floor was carpeted with wood shavings and every piece of furniture was garnished with the dust that had seeped in from the workshop. They sat at a long oak kitchen table and quenched their thirst.

'Are you going to arrest me?' Bernard asked happily.

'What for?' Pel replied seriously.

'Oh, I don't know, but I'm sure we could find something – a parking ticket I haven't paid, *pourquoi pas*?'

'Parking tickets aren't our problem,' Pel said accepting another glass of water, 'but your ex-wife, Jacqueline – '

'Oh hell, what's she done now, driven up a lamppost in a state of deep inebriation?'

'Not that I know of, but she was in Avignon driving her father around in a white Nevada brake. She says you lent it to her.'

'I did, and I shouldn't have. She caught the back of it on a bollard reversing out of a hotel car-park, or at least so she says, and I'm going to have to pay for a new optic. I regret the day I met that one.'

'But you married her,' Darras pointed out.

'We declared *concubinage*,' Bernard corrected, 'it's not quite the same, but I see what you mean. She was gorgeous once, before the wine took over and destroyed her. I threw her out three years ago when I couldn't stand her drunken parties any longer – that and the boyfriends were just too much. She changed men as often as she changed her underwear. Finding her in bed with her brother-in-law was the last straw.'

'Which one?'

'François, Lorette's husband. Nice enough chap but not too bright with women – he didn't stand a chance, it would have been her who made the immoral suggestions. Mind you, she'd already tried it on with Jean-Paul, Maxine's husband, but he told me he wouldn't play. He told François to watch out too, but he didn't listen.'

'Friends, are they, the two brothers-in-law?'

'Not what I'd call friends, they're so different, one's a peasant the other one never breathes fresh air except to go fishing on his very private lake with his very private colleagues, but they get on okay at family gatherings. I don't suppose they have much choice in the matter.'

'And the latest boyfriend?'

'Don't know him, don't want to.'

'Monsieur, could you tell me where you were between dusk on Monday and dawn on Tuesday of this week?'

'Bloody hell, I'm not sure I could even tell you what I was doing yesterday.' However, after a struggle with his memory, it was established that he'd been having a meal with the client who'd ordered the massive bookcase. 'I think it was that evening I went round to measure up, we got talking and I stayed to eat. Check with him to be certain.'

On their way out Pel stopped to admire a very fine desk sitting in the corner of the room. It was small and delicately made, obviously created by a master cabinet-maker. It was the sort of desk his wife would like.

'Where did you buy it?' he asked.

'You like it?'

'I believe my wife would.'

'I'll make you one,' Bernard said simply.

'You made that?' Pel was surprised, he'd thought the desk was an antique.

Bernard nodded, removing his hands from his pockets and turning them over. They were as huge as a couple of blunt shovels. 'These', he said, 'are exquisite tools.'

Pel turned over the facts of Josephe Blau's death in his mind; it had changed his attitude to the entertaining hold-up at the airport. It meant they might never find out what had been stolen, unless they caught the clever devils that had done the stealing, and a fat chance they had of that, unless they knew where to look, in other words, knew what had been stolen. Had old Blau's eyes and mouth closed for ever because he had nothing left to live for? Or had he been shut up deliberately? Pel was still looking for the elusive piece to fit in the puzzle.

While he was with Bernard, Nosjean and Brochard had arrived at the farm near Ste Etienne where they found Jacqueline's boyfriend John Willis, alone and polishing a gleaming Harley Davidson. He was a tall, well-built man with long blond hair and a large cross hanging from one ear. He was dressed in black from head to foot, apparently unaware of the suffocating heat, and on the back of his T-shirt was a large skull and crossbones.

'Hi, guys,' he called as they came towards him across the grubby yard. 'Lost, are you?'

They both flipped open their identification. The easily

111

recognisable red, white and blue stripe changed his attitude immediately.

'Hey, what's up? My papers are in order, you can't touch me, I'm a citizen of the United States of America with a valid visa to visit Europe.'

'It's about Monsieur Blau's death,' Nosjean explained, eyeing the monkey wrench in the biker's hand.

'Oh, sure.' Willis relaxed and went back to his shining motor bike. 'Jackie rang me to tell me she was stuck in Avignon with her dad, I went out for a spin on the bike. Dogs and goats are fine,' he said without looking up, 'but they're not great conversationalists. There are a few Angels that hang out in town so I pissed off to see if I could find them. Had a couple of drinks then we came back here for the night, can't remember much more but I know we sank a lot of bourbon.'

He did manage to remember the name of the bar where he'd found the other bikers; and when Nosjean asked the owner, he remembered the evening well, complaining about losing his regular customers to the loud Hell's Angels. Although he couldn't identify Willis by name he did describe 'a big bloke with long blond hair and a sodding great crucifix hanging from his ear' as being the rowdiest.

De Troq' had been checking Maxine's story of a dinner party with her husband Jean-Paul.

'I told her to stop fussing,' he said. '*Mon Dieu*, we've had her father living with us ever since we were married, it'd been wonderful to have the house to ourselves while he was in hospital. He had his own apartment in our house, but he also had an electric bell that he pressed whenever he needed anything. He enjoyed that bell. It was bliss without the old codger. I got to know my wife again, I'd planned our first dinner party without him for years, and he goes and disappears again. Well, I was buggered if he was going to spoil the evening. I took the mobile phone into my study, put it beside the answering machine and closed the door on both.'

Their guests confirmed they'd been to the Rolland-Blaus' for dinner and complimented Jean-Paul on his cooking. 'He's a wonderful husband,' one woman said, 'so thoughtful and attentive. As we left he was insisting she left everything to him and went straight to bed.'

Lorette claimed to have been at home while her husband, François, had gone out. That was as much as she'd say on the phone so Bardolle and Pujol set off once again for the Mâcon district.

Out of earshot of his wife, François readily admitted he'd been with a woman in Villefranche but refused to give them her name. However, he did say they'd eaten at the Toque Blanche restaurant. 'They'll remember me, I'm sure,' he said. 'I knocked a vase of flowers clean off the table.'

Lorette admitted that once François was out of the way, her manager had come over to the house to go over the accounts. When Bardolle repeated this to him, he hooted with laughter. 'So that's what she calls it, is it? Heaven knows why she lied, not to protect François, they don't give a damn about each other – and anyway,' he said as if it justified his adultery, 'he's at it too.'

The team had been thorough, right down to the young waitress who'd mopped up the water at the feet of François. Everyone had been where they said they'd been. Pensively, Pel took a cigarette from the small blue packet and considered the Blau family. Did he have an over-suspicious mind? He inhaled deeply, slowly turning the pages of the file. The old man's door had been locked, the manager had had to open it and had followed Jacqueline into the room, she'd found her father Blau dead between the sheets and had hysterics, the manager had calmed her down and called for the police. When they'd given permission, he'd removed the other key from the bedside

113

table. The door had been locked from the inside. The heart pills were found under the bed; they'd been there all the time. Had Blau dropped them and been too tired to retrieve them? Or had he forgotten them completely, woken in a panic, reached out in the dark and knocked them on the floor – but it was already too late, his heart was already going into spasm? Whichever way Pel looked at it, reluctantly he had to admit the inquest would return the verdict of accidental death. Slowly he closed the file and pushed it away.

10

Pel was sure he'd missed something. Although he went over and over it in the car on the way home, leaving a trail of exasperated motorists behind him, the missing piece still evaded him and he arrived home sporting a deep frown ready to do battle with Madame Routy.

His wife greeted him at the door; she was jubilant. 'I've found it,' she said, kissing him on the cheek, 'just what I've been looking for. It's in a bit of a mess but not irretrievable.'

'I'm delighted,' Pel replied, picking up the Gameboy, disappointed that he couldn't surprise her with the pretty desk he'd seen at Bernard's.

Madame Routy came into the sitting-room to join in Madame's pleasure and the chattering of the two women broke his concentration. He switched off the little grey box and resignedly switched on a smile. Madame Routy took two steps back. She knew Pel's smiles, they weren't nice. He glared at her and at last she disappeared completely.

He put his arm round his wife as she sat on the arm of his chair. She explained that her excitement was due to a clock, a grandfather clock, she'd been searching for for months. Blast, Pel sighed, and I thought it was a desk she was after. It was a good thing he hadn't told her about his find.

'I'm so thrilled,' Madame was saying, 'I've even found a clockmaker to renovate the face and make it tick prettily. All I've got to do is locate an *ébéniste* to do the *cerisier* casing.'

Pel brightened. 'I know just the man,' he said.

'How wonderful.' She hugged him affectionately. 'My

dear, I'm a very lucky woman to have such a knowledge-able husband.'

Pel was startled by her statement but leapt at the opportunity of keeping his wife happy. 'We should cele-brate,' he suggested. 'I'll tell Madame Routy we're eating out tonight.'

And with uncontrollable pleasure he made his announcement in the kitchen to a red-faced and angry housekeeper who'd been busily preparing their meal most of the afternoon. She'd been remarkably trained since his marriage but he hadn't forgotten the burnt offerings she served him before his wife came into their lives and never missed a chance at revenge. It was rare, but very sweet.

Pel slipped quietly up the staircase towards his office. So far he hadn't crossed paths with one of his team and he was hoping to arrive unnoticed to nurse his indigestion without interruption. He and his wife had had a delicious meal with an excellent bottle of Nuits St Georges, they'd even indulged in an Armagnac with their coffee, but he'd slept badly as usual and was convinced his non-existent ulcer was about to explode because of his excesses. Any minute now he'd be carted off to hospital to be operated on, then what would the Hôtel de Police do? All he wanted was a couple of the Citrate de Bétaine tablets he kept in his desk drawer and soon everything would be back to normal. He opened his door, making as little sound as possible, closed it and, placing a cigarette between his lips, lit the first glorious Gauloise of the day.

'Tobacco is responsible for sixty-six thousand deaths in France every year; fifty-five thousand from cancer and another eleven thousand from *cardio-vasculaire* disease.'

The voice of Leguyder, the walking encyclopaedia, made him spin round. He was the last person in the world Pel wanted to see, knowing it would take hours of long

116

words and patience to get rid of the man from Forensics. He took a long suck on his nerve-calmer; checking his scowl was firmly in place, he strolled over to his chair, sat, pushed his glasses up into the remains of his hair and prepared himself for the inevitable.

'It is also responsible for many dangerous illnesses, asthma, bronchitis – '

'And it is responsible for well over twenty-three million francs of revenue for the government,' Pel retorted, 'and although I think Chirac should be shot, I'm a loyal Frenchman and must contribute to the economy.'

Leguyder snorted. 'The cost of treating illnesses caused by tobacco costs the country forty-five million, so that excuse is as stupid as smoking.'

'Never mind about my smoking, what do you want?' Pel was anxious to get his hands on his indigestion tablets but didn't dare risk it in front of Leguyder, it would mean another three-hour lecture.

'The box that was stolen from the plane,' Leguyder said opening a depressingly hefty file. 'I still have it in the lab. It is made of pine and is 96 centimetres long, 66 centimetres wide and 36 centimetres high,' he read. 'With its lid and the packing inside it weighs 4.95 kilos. When it was checked in at Montpellier it weighed 32.1 kilos and was supposed to contain a number of bottles of perfume.'

Pel sighed. Leguyder hadn't told him anything new yet, but he went on listening, certain that he'd come to the point eventually.

'Now, deducting the weight of the crate and packing from the delivered weight we find that 27.15 kilos of merchandise had been removed. I've tried with all sorts of bottles filled with water and I'm telling you it was impossible, there simply isn't enough space for that much perfume.'

'We'd worked that out already,' Pel said, 'and anyway the perfume samples were found at the factory.'

'Oh, thank you for keeping me informed.' Leguyder's sarcasm was lost on Pel. He looked in pain but was only stifling a yawn. 'What was removed', Leguyder continued, 'was relatively small considering the weight.'

'Darcy suggested scrap metal.'

'He wasn't that far from the truth,' the scientist said triumphantly. 'We've experimented with hundreds of possibilities, all trying to look like bags of potatoes, and I think I can safely say I've come up with the correct answer.'

Pel thought he might have. 'Well?' he said. 'What was in the box?'

'Gold coins in small pouches, placed in larger sacks.'

So now they knew, finally they'd cracked it, thanks to the painstaking calculations of Leguyder. Unfortunately, instead of helping, it only complicated matters, but it did alter the situation slightly. Gold had always been a very good reason for lies, robbery and murder. Back to square one and rejuggle all the pieces to see if this time they'd fall in a straight line pointing them in the right direction.

Pel waded his way through the statements and stories. By the end of the day he was sick to death of the Blau family; the only one he'd liked was the old boy and he was dead. Why had he been shipping gold to Burgundy? It must have been worth ten times, a hundred times, the perfume he'd hidden in the cupboard, but how much? He decided to call in his personal expert, the Baron de Troquereau. Blast him, Pel was always envious of his title, but as de Troq's highly polished shoes insinuated themselves through his door, Pel glanced down at his own scuffed suede-covered feet: it was no good, being a baron took generations of practice, it was too late for the Pels.

'Well?' he shouted at the immaculate detective who still looked too young to be out of school.

'Very well, thank you,' de Troq' replied, smiling. 'My presence was requested, I believe.'

'Oh, sit down, shut up and tell me about your family fortune.'

'There isn't one, Patron.'

'But there was once,' Pel insisted.

'Indeed there was.'

'Did you have any gold coins?'

'We've still got one or two.'

'I hope you keep them under lock and key.'

'Until recently they were kept in the traditional place, stuffed into old clogs and hidden up the chimney. But when I became a policeman my mother was persuaded that perhaps they'd be safer in the bank.'

'I'm glad to hear it,' Pel said. 'Now, tell me, how much are they worth?'

'That depends on the condition of the coin, the year it was made and where it was made. But', he went on, noticing Pel fidgeting with impatience, 'a *louis d'or*, for instance, can be worth from as little as four hundred francs to as much as fourteen thousand.'

'That's quite a difference,' Pel agreed. 'So would it be possible to work out how much thirty kilos of them could be worth?'

'Without seeing them, no. Do you know their age? Are you really talking about *louis d'or* or *napoléons*?'

Pel ran his hand through his non-existent hair. 'Leguyder told me this morning that the bags lifted from the plane must have contained gold coins. I shan't tell you how he knows because he lost me half-way through his explanation, but while he's a crashing bore, he's very competent and doesn't make mistakes. If he says they were gold coins I'm prepared to believe him.'

'But they might not have been old,' de Troq' pointed out. 'Gold coins are still made. There's a five-hundred franc one to commemorate de Gaulle, another for Dwight

Eisenhower, another for Sir Winston Churchill – they're only a few years old. But they're worth about three thousand francs already,' he added. 'The Voltaire that came out in 1994 is worth five thousand.'

'Holy Mother of God!' Pel was rapidly becoming exasperated by it all. To change the conversation slightly he fished in his pocket and threw the contents on to the desk: three one-franc pieces and a few centimes. 'Go on,' he said, 'tell me what that's worth.'

De Troq' turned the coins over. '1992, one franc,' he said, 'worth one franc. 1976, if it was in perfect condition, worth fifteen. Ah, 1966, if it was *fleur de coin*, i.e. unused, it'd be worth sixty.'

'You seem to know a lot about it,' Pel commented.

'I got involved with the clogs up the chimney and catalogued the whole lot before mother would hand over her inheritance to the bank.'

'How much did it weigh?'

'Each clog contained around two kilos.'

'So tell me about how much thirty kilos is worth.'

'The current value is around four hundred American dollars an ounce,' de Troq' said as he picked up the calculator on the desk, 'so that would represent about two million francs. But antique coins like mother's ...' He shrugged, putting the little machine down again. 'That's anybody's guess. Ten million?' he suggested. 'Could be more.'

Pel whistled. '*Merde alors*,' he managed. 'You'd better start guessing, I want to know approximately what we're talking about. How would they dispose of the stuff?'

'If they wanted the real value they'd have to sell piece by piece to a numismatist.'

'Are there a lot of them about?'

'Over fifty members of the Syndicat National des Experts here in France.'

'De Troq', fax every one of them, then get on to the

heads of all the other European syndicates, particularly in the countries touching the borders of France, and tell them to keep their eyes open. If Leguyder is right, someone will want to sell, either now or in the near future. And de Troq',' Pel added thoughtfully, 'don't tell anyone else, specially Misset.'

'I never tell Misset anything, Patron.'

'Good thing too. It's now six weeks since they held up the plane. They know we know it wasn't perfume they stole, even if that's what they expected, but they don't know we do know it's gold. They'll be getting cocky at pulling off the perfect robbery; any minute now they'll make a move and we'll have them. The Chief, Darcy and Nosjean must be informed, but for the moment no one else.'

'What abut Leguyder and the lab technicians?'

'I'll have a word with him. He may be boring but he's trustworthy.'

But as de Troq' left his office Pel was frowning hard. He was considering the facts and they still didn't fit together properly. What the hell was a Polish refugee, who'd managed to escape death by the skin of his teeth, doing with all that gold? If they turned out to be relatively new coins he could have bought them, he'd become a wealthy man. But old gold ... Pel decided that was improbable. In his experience, however, the improbable was always possible.

11

With the body of her father at last released, Maxine put her efficient hand to organising his funeral and to everyone's surprise it took place on 25th August in a small village in Burgundy not far from Beauzile. This apparently had been his wish.

Pel was present, accompanied by de Troq' and Misset, who was only there to keep him out of trouble while the rest of the team got on with their work unhampered by having the fading James Bond leering over their shoulders.

It was another boiling day. The countryside shimmered in the heat as they followed the cortège that crawled from the little church along the winding lanes to the graveyard three kilometres outside the village. The mass of black ribbons hung limply from the undertaker's car and the smell of incense clung sickeningly to their clothes.

Gathering round an open tomb waiting for the coffin to descend into its cold yawning mouth was always pretty cheerless, even when the coffin contained an old man who'd had a respectably long life filled with success. The only thing that brightened the scene were the colourful summer dresses the women were wearing. Maxine was particularly striking in a scarlet outfit, while her husband, Jean-Paul, standing at her side puffing gently on a small cigar, looked distinguished in his expensive suit. He didn't seem to be suffering from the blistering heat like Pel, who could feel the perspiration breaking out in rivers all over him.

As they listened to the priest's droning voice, Pel could stand it no longer; turning to look for a patch of shade, he saw there wasn't a single tree in the enclosed graveyard. However, he did see an ancient Citroën Traction arrive at the gates. A man of about his own age got out and helped an elderly lady from the passenger's seat. Agonisingly slowly they began the long walk to the graveside. The man's face was baked a deep brown with well-furrowed skin from a peasant's life; he was tall and thin, and moved uneasily inside his carefully pressed Sunday clothes. The woman he escorted was even thinner but proudly erect, possessing a tangible dignity beneath her elaborate black hat. They stopped and watched the proceedings a little way from the small crowd. Pel wasn't sure, but felt it was worth a try.

As the priest came to the end of his little speech, the daughters stepped forward to scatter a handful of earth on the descending coffin, and with the help of her son the old woman turned away.

Pel walked a few steps behind until they were out of earshot of the other mourners. 'Mariette,' he called quietly.

She stopped immediately and hesitatingly turned towards him. 'My name, monsieur, is Antoinette Latour,' she replied with a soft trembling voice.

'Excuse me, madame, but I think you were once known as Mariette.'

'That was a long time ago. A friend added Marie to my name making me sound like the wife of Louis XVI. It became shortened to Mariette,' she explained and turned again towards the Citroën. 'If you wish to speak to me, I must invite you to accompany me into the interior of my motor car. I'm unable to stand for long.'

Once they were seated on the leather upholstery, with the doors firmly closed against the now advancing procession of mourners, she lifted the black veil from her face and looked Pel in the eye. In spite of her age her slanting dark brown eyes were bright, sitting in nests of wrinkles made from a clear pale complexion. She would have been beautiful in her youth.

'Yes,' she said, 'Mariette is a name I have been called but I shall never be called that again.'

Pel chose his words carefully, not wanting to offend this dignified old lady. 'Then you knew the Polish refugee before he escaped at the end of the war?'

For a moment she looked confused, then a small smile creased her lined face. 'Yes, I met him once or twice.'

'Madame, forgive me for my indiscretion but it is important for our investigations into a robbery at Dijon airport. I have reason to believe that perhaps what was stolen had something to do with you. I must ask you if you were his lover.'

'No, monsieur, I was not,' she said firmly.

'Josephe Blau had two books inscribed "With love from Mariette" and dated 1945, St Beauzile. How did they come into his possession?'

Madame Latour smiled modestly. 'When one is young,' she said, 'one makes impulsive gestures. Later when it has come to an end sometimes they are regretted. He must have been given them by someone believing he would appreciate them.'

'It wasn't you?'

'Monsieur, I may be poor, but I am not in the habit of handing out my affections to Polish refugees.'

Scratching his head, Pel thanked her and left the car. He stood watching it disappear slowly into the afternoon dust. He'd found Mariette but it hadn't helped at all; he still didn't know any more about the gold or where it had been headed after the bank in the city.

He considered the possibility that Madame Latour had been lying, but he was inclined to doubt it. Her eyes hadn't left his as she answered his questions. The more he pondered, the more he was sure she'd been telling the truth. But he was also sure that there was more to it and that he'd missed a vital fact again.

As requested, Maxine telephoned Pel at the office after the reading of the will and confirmed that there had been no surprises. Blau's remaining part in Blau Beauté plus his belongings at the château were hers; the rest of his estate, which was still considerable, was to be 'divided equally between all living issue of the deceased'.

Pel noticed there had been no mention of Mariette. Perhaps the two books had been nothing but a red herring and she had nothing to do with the old boy after all – but, he said to himself, she'd gone to his funeral.

Fearing the worst, he decided Maxine had to be told about the real contents of the stolen crate but her reply was surprisingly calm; she pointed out that they didn't know he had it so it made no difference to have lost it. He expected some reaction from the other two sisters but there was none. They were an odd bunch.

Towards the end of the day de Troq' came into his office with Debray, who was carrying a sheaf of papers covered with numbers. He silently placed it before Pel, who looked at it briefly.

'It looks like a train timetable to me,' he said, running his finger down one of the columns, 'with the station names missing, totally incomprehensible. Translate.'

'I've been checking on gold coins, Patron,' de Troq' explained. 'I did the rounds of the banks on the south coast that Monsieur Blau could have dealt with, plus those in our own city, to see if he ordered the commemorative coins issued in the last twenty years. They were limited editions and were spread around all over France. To have had enough to weigh nearly thirty kilos he would have had to order them from a number of banks, but I came up with a complete negative, he showed no interest in new coins at all. So we assume they were old ones. I checked with the numismatic societies and they don't know him either, so he didn't buy them as a collector. They keep careful records of transactions, so he must have had them for a long time.'

'Since the war?'

'It looks likely.'

'Where the hell would a Polish refugee find bags of gold?'

'We wondered about that too,' Debray said, 'but you know the Germans stole and hoarded an enormous amount of treasure. When the war was turning against them, they grabbed everything they could and ran. It's possible Blau came across a cache that had been forgotten in their panic to get back to Germany and took it for himself.'

'Thirty kilos is a hell of a lot for one man to carry all the way to Sète,' Pel pointed out.

'British soldiers went into battle in 1914 carrying sixty-six pounds of equipment on their backs,' de Troq' said. 'That's the equivalent of thirty kilos – and they were fighting, not simply carrying it.'

'Point taken,' Pel agreed. 'Go on.'

'As I told you, in terms of gold at today's market price, the bandits got away with nearly two million francs' worth.'

It was a large sum of money, although not astonishing.

'However,' Debray referred to their calculations, 'if the gold was old coins of say ten, twenty or forty francs, like the ones de Troq's mother has, they weigh up to ten grams and – '

'If they're in perfect condition, *flan bruni*, we're talking in terms of fifty million.'

'That's one hell of a lot of money to make no difference to three sisters.'

126

'Do they know its value?'

Pel was busy scribbling on his notepad. 'They didn't ask,' he said. A seed of doubt was easing its way into his mind.

Two days later, Pel stormed into the morning meeting. 'Right,' he bellowed, 'let's have it. Where were they all on the day of the robbery? We'll start with your report, Misset.'

Misset dropped his notes on the floor and, in his panic to retrieve them, dropped his sun-glasses. After a lot of shuffling and groaning he came to life.

'Jacqueline and Willis were at a rock concert,' he said.

'In the middle of the week?' Pel shouted at him, immediately suspicious.

'It was a private party. The hosts told me they are members of a rock band and their guests were mostly unemployed. Jacqueline and Willis arrived around midday in the Ban the Bomb van in time for the meal and were there when the music started that evening. They left late the following morning.'

'Thank you, Misset, you can go back to sleep,' Pel said. 'Bardolle, you next.'

'Lorette didn't want to tell me but the manager did; they set off together for a wine convention in Paris but spent most of the day in bed at a motel on the Périphé-rique. I checked, the concierge noticed the black and white couple.'

'And François?'

'He was seen before lunch in a bar outside Beaune and again later that afternoon having spent an unsuccessful day in town trying to find a new girlfriend.' Pujol had rushed it a bit, but had managed not to stammer enough to allow Pel to interrupt him.

'Rings true,' Misset commented.

'You'd know all about chasing skirts in Beaune, of course – perhaps you should give the poor bloke a few tips.' Pel took his glasses off and started polishing them on his shirt front. 'Go on, surprise me, where were Mad Max and the smooth Jean-Paul?'

'Maxine spent the day at a health club sorting out her cellulite,' Nosjean said; 'they confirm her appointment, and Jean-Paul went fishing with friends, although they say he didn't catch much.'

'Where?'

'A private lake at St Seine l'Abbaye.'

'Near here?'

'He was driven from the city by Monsieur Burais, having left his own car in an underground car-park. The same *type* took him to collect it the following day. His bank account shows he paid for the overnight stay with his banker's card, and the motorway from Sète and back to Séte the following day was paid for by the same bit of plastic. He was seen on and off at the lakeside all day by Burais and was there for the celebrations in the *abri de pêcheur* that evening.'

Back in his own office, Pel reread the reports in full. When he'd finished he flung his biro across the room in fury. The Blau family's movements were well and truly accounted for, they always were.

'Damn, blast and hellfire,' he muttered to himself, 'I don't bloody believe it!'

He pressed the intercom. 'Pujol! Get in here and take this file away from me. Check the timings, all of them, to the second. No one else could have known about that gold except for the family. One of them's got to be involved.'

12

During the last week of the long summer holidays the bodies on the beach, desperately trying to deepen their tans before returning to the cities, were forced to take cover in their frail summer homes, nailing everything to the floor and blocking all openings to their shelters. Children's buckets and spades were used for bailing out instead of building sandcastles. The heavens clothed themselves in colours fit for a funeral and proceeded to pour millions of gallons of rain on to the despairing holiday-makers. The wind howled, demolishing the flimsy canvas homes and pushing caravans on to their sides, rivers swelled and gushed over into the parched fields, trees fell bringing with them electric cables and telephone lines, the Atlantic and Mediterranean looked like angry black soup. The summer was suddenly over; streams of cars left the seaside filled with undercooked families, drenched and disheartened.

The farmers looked out gloomily as enormous scars of devastation were cut into their crops and the *vignerons* who'd been looking forward to a bumper crop of grapes started shaking their heads and watching for mould creeping into the vineyards.

When the schoolchildren picked up their satchels at the beginning of a new school year they also picked up their raincoats and sou'westers. The temperature dropped and fires were lit. Winter had arrived; autumn hadn't happened.

Pel was depressed. Staring out at the non-stop torrent beyond his window, he decided that he hated weather. There was far too much of it, and this was the worst kind.

The mornings were grey and cold, the days filled with tramping about in soggy shoes, fighting against the driving rain. They'd solved a number of cases in the millions they had on file; he, Darcy, de Troq' and Bardolle had appeared in court prior to seeing a few of their old friends disappear for a short stay in prison, but as far as the bullion robbery – because that was what it was – at the airport was concerned, they'd been less than productive. Even the motorway accident was still a mystery to them.

Nosjean had been worrying him too. Pel had an idea it was not going too well for him at home, but dared not interfere; he could barely cope with his own marriage, never mind sort out the problems of someone else's.

Darcy on the other hand was nauseating. He was more handsome than ever, making Pel feel like an old toad. His teeth sparkled whiter than white every time he grinned, which was often, and he'd been caught singing in the corridors of the Hôtel de Police. It had got to be stopped, such merriment was enough to put Pel off his Gauloises.

He watched the evening closing in, bringing a chilling darkness that lingered until the music of the downpour drumming constantly on the roof woke him at dawn.

The *vendange* began and every day going towards the city Pel saw peasants fighting a losing battle with the elements, gathering their grapes in the hope that the wine wouldn't be too diluted with rainwater. The slow tractors pulling trailers full of sodden crops slid in and out of the fields holding up traffic more than usual on the mud-covered country roads. During the grape harvest the air was usually filled with the intoxicating yeasty smell of wine fermenting, but that year all they smelt was wet earth.

Everyone was grumbling; tourism had had its worst year for decades, *la grippe* was already running amok filling the doctors' waiting rooms to overflowing and of course the farmers were talking of ruin. The government promised help; there were a few laughs but not many. Pel's team weren't much more jolly than the drenched bands of pickers in the vineyards.

The small but constant ray of sunshine in Pel's dismal life was his wife. The cabinet-maker, Bernard, had telephoned to say that the grandfather clock was finished; they were invited to see the work of art.

'I'll pick you up tomorrow afternoon,' Madame Pel said, smiling happily at him. 'We'll go and see it together.'

'I expect it'll be raining,' Pel replied gloomily.

'So we'll get wet!'

He ran across the street with his mackintosh over his head and a couple of boys sheltering in a doorway started singing 'Batman, dada, dada, Batman' at the tops of their voices. He scowled at them, caught his foot on the kerbstone and nearly fell flat on his face in a puddle, much to their amusement. Collapsing through the open door of his wife's Twingo, he stared at his saturated socks and his misshapen shoes awash with gallons of ungodly rain.

'I got wet,' he said.

Having sorted out her dripping detective, his wife started the engine and drove him calmly out of the city. He sat inconsolably beside her, turning the facts of too many cases over in his mind. He was so deep in thought that when Bernard opened his door for him, he was startled.

'What are you doing here?' he demanded.

'Hoping you'll decide to get out so we can all go inside.'

The clockmaker was at Madame's side holding a large but dripping umbrella. 'Come on, Pel,' she said kindly, 'for a short half-hour you can switch off being a policeman and throw yourself into being an enthusiastic husband.'

Pel was shocked – husband he might be, enthusiastic

131

occasionally, but throwing himself anywhere was quite out of the question. However he followed her into the house and tried to concentrate on what they'd come for. He felt like a schoolboy on an outing to the local museum, an interested expression pinned to his face but unable to understand a word that was being said. At least he wouldn't have to write an essay on it later. It was a small consolation.

He had to admit though that the clock was magnificent; the two craftsmen were proud of their work. His wife was thrilled and, having stroked its fine polished wood and listened to its chime, she started talking money. Pel felt faint as he watched the large wad of banknotes change hands.

They opened a bottle of champagne and toasted the transaction, delivery being promised the moment the weather changed. No one wanted to spoil the masterpiece with rain stains.

As they were leaving Bernard commented to Pel that his ex-wife had been pestering him for the loan of his car again. 'She says it's for a trip up north,' he said, 'and called me all the names under the sun when I said no.'

'Where up north?'

'I haven't a clue. She's going with her boyfriend, she said, to share the driving, so it must be quite a way. *De toute façon.*' He laughed. 'She'll have to stop at Dieppe, there's nothing but water after that.'

Pel was silent on the way back: after Dieppe there was nothing but water, until you hit England. Willis was American, that meant he spoke English; England was renowned for its knowledge of antiques and it was one of the largest money markets in the world. He knew he was clutching at straws but he had to clutch at something.

He got in touch with Chief Inspector Goschen of Scotland Yard, who'd helped them in the past. After a surprisingly cordial greeting, Goschen suggested they got

132

down to business and Pel panicked. He ran out of the office in search of de Troq', whose aristocratic upbringing meant that speaking foreign languages came naturally to him, whereas Pel was restricted to a very limited vocabulary that was enhanced only by facial expressions and a lot of gesticulating with his hands, which wasn't much good on the phone.

De Troq' carefully explained to the patient Englishman what Pel suspected and finally put the phone down again.

'He'll get back to you if he has any news. He's going to get in touch with Spinks of London to see if they've had any contact with someone from France wanting to sell old coins.'

Pel sighed with relief; now perhaps they'd see some action.

When Goschen rang back the following morning it didn't look likely. Spinks, the coin dealers, had confirmed they'd had a number of foreign enquiries but none specifically involving a large collection for sale. They'd been reminded of the fax sent earlier in the year, as had all other numismatists in England. Goschen did, however, confirm finding John Willis, the American, in the British police records. He'd been picked up on suspicion of importing marijuana into the country from Holland the previous year, but while he smelt strongly of the drug not a trace was found on him. Goschen apologised for not being more encouraging and rang off.

So they were back to the waiting game.

On 27th September the rain stopped, Pel's men removed their swimming goggles and finally furled their tortured umbrellas. It was a start. At the beginning of October the sun oozed lazily out from behind the retreating clouds

133

and made the countryside steam. Women and children were seen on the streets again, cafés put their tables and chairs back on the pavements and the students at the university pegged themselves out half naked in the park to contemplate life in the now boiling sunshine. But Pel was still depressed. There had been no news from the numismatists anywhere. The Blau family were keeping a low profile and behaving perfectly normally. He had to take it out on someone: Misset as always was the perfect candidate.

He was slumped in his chair in the sergeants' room staring at a report. It was early and, watching him through the open door, Pel decided he must be waiting for someone to come and switch him on.

'Slouching again, Misset?' he bellowed.

'Trying to work something out, Patron,' Misset answered lethargically.

'The plug is right behind you,' Pel said sadistically.

'*Comment?*'

'For your brain, man, you need to plug it in.'

Pel felt slightly better and stormed back out, slamming the door behind him, and succeeding in rattling the panes of glass as if an earthquake had followed him into the corridor.

Half an hour later Darcy came into his office looking like Prince Charming. Pel felt worse again and attacked a new packet of cigarettes.

'Patron, something interesting's come up,' Darcy said. 'You know Misset spends a lot of time dreaming in the office to keep out of his wife's hair?'

'He shouldn't,' Pel replied puffing viciously.

'This time, it's a good thing he did. The report on the two getaway cars had gone missing, I'd given it to him to file but instead he'd put it in his desk.'

'Fire him!'

'Hang on.' Darcy smiled. 'He has the habit of taking it

out and opening it every time he hears footsteps in the corridor, in the vain hope that whoever comes through the door will think he's working. He's turned its pages so often now that they're getting very dog-eared. Personally I'm surprised that he's read a word of it but apparently he has – he knows the thing off by heart. In one of the cars a number of cigarette stubs, Marlboro and Gauloises, were found – nothing surprising in that, everyone smokes them. In the other, stubs of Marlboro and a couple of cigar ends. That is surprising because at the back of the file is the statement of the owner of the second car. He doesn't smoke although his wife does. But I doubt very much that she indulges in cigars.'

Pel was beginning to look interested.

'Leguyder, being thorough in his work, had noted that the cigar stubs were small King Edwards. Misset tells me they're not easily found in France but can be bought at airports.'

'Trust Misset to know that.'

'There's more,' Darcy went on. 'He's sure he came across someone smoking King Edwards recently and has been racking his brain to remember who and where. He just did – it was Mad Max's husband, Jean-Paul, at Blau's funeral.'

'Holy Mother of God! It sounds like something out of a Tintin annual, any minute now we'll have Captain Haddock on our hands too.' But Pel's memory was working overtime. 'The old man was smoking a small cigar when we saw him at the château,' he remembered, 'and Mad Max said he'd have to give up pinching them from her husband because of his heart condition. *Eh bien*, it's not a lot but it's better than nothing. Tell Misset to unplug his brain again before he blows a fuse.'

'If Jean-Paul has a permanent supply it means he travels a lot, so I found out from his secretary where she books his tickets and discovered he'd been in Strasbourg in July and London at the beginning of August. However, the two trips were apparently innocent; Strasbourg was to see his brother, and the company in Swindon, England, spent two days with him discussing launching the Blau Beauté products on the English market before declining to sign an over-expensive contract. By the way, they all think I'm a market researcher, Jean-Paul doesn't know I've been asking questions.'

'Where is he now? I wouldn't mind having a word with him myself.'

Darcy frowned. 'I can't locate him.'

'What about his wife, Mad Max, and the rest of them?'

As Darcy left Pel's office the phone trilled on his desk.

It was Bernard, the cabinet-maker. 'How's the clock?' he asked cheerfully.

'Ticking,' Pel replied absent-mindedly, still thinking about what Darcy had told him.

'Look,' Bernard persevered, 'this is probably not important and I'll apologise for wasting your time, but I think the bitch has stolen my car.'

'*Accouche.*'

'I went out to the workshop early this morning, it must have been around half-past seven, it was still dark, and when I came in a few minutes ago the garage doors across the yard were yawning at me, no car. I can't imagine your ordinary car thief would bother coming all this way down miles of country lanes.'

'You'd be surprised,' Pel said, 'but on the other hand, she could easily have had doubles made of your keys the last time.'

Pel dialled Jacqueline's number, only to be told by France Telecom that it was no longer in service, she hadn't paid her bill. Darcy dropped what he was doing and, dragging a sulking Misset behind him, went to find a car to take them to the goat farm at Ste Etienne.

Unfortunately it was market day again and the traffic was crawling through streets stuffed with pedestrians. It was the first sunny market day for a month and the inhabitants from far and wide were crammed into the centre of the city, clonking their overflowing baskets against the car.

'Come on, darling, five kilos of tomatoes for the price of one!' The coarse voice of a stall-holder cut through the crowd and pierced Pel's thoughts. He scowled at her. 'Yes, you, darling, last of the season, it's now or next year.'

He tried to ignore her stare as she persevered in her attempt to harpoon his interest but it was impossible. Finally he called back, 'I'll take fifty if you can clear the sodding traffic.'

She wiped her solid hands on a grubby apron and waded across to them with ten trays of tomatoes which she deposited with a heavy thump on the bonnet of the car. '*Marché conclu*,' she said triumphantly, pushing her open hand through the open window. Pel looked bewildered, then he looked at Darcy, who shrugged and dug into his pocket for the money. Misset was told to deal with the tomatoes, and while he slowly loaded them into the boot, the stall-holder started screaming at the seething throng.

'Come on, you lot, get a move on, the Mayor's coming through!'

For a moment there was no response until the other market sellers caught on and screamed with her. It was terrifying. Pel wanted to hide under his seat with embarrassment but by the time Misset had installed the last tray, a narrow passage had opened up through the sea of bodies. Darcy gently put his foot on the accelerator. Pel

137

turned in his seat to see his sergeant cantering behind them trying to slam the boot closed and open the back door while avoiding trampling on the lingering peasants who were attempting to squeeze themselves on to the packed pavements. For a moment he was lost from view, having tripped splendidly over a wheelbarrow and scattered thousands of apples all over the cobblestones. He reappeared, his head down and going like an overweight Olympic athlete, and managed to fling himself in behind Pel and Darcy while the apple owner was yelling for a policeman.

'Clumsy clot,' Pel said, stifling a smile. It had been the best thing he'd seen in days.

The herd of goats looked up as they stopped outside the dilapidated farmhouse. Two dogs howled on the ends of chains; the others barked frantically from behind a collapsing barn door. The Ban the Bomb van was sitting in a heap of rusting metal. Darcy leaned on the horn, sending the dogs wild; he banged on the door and tried the knob, but it was locked and there was no reply. Fiddling his fingers under a rotting shutter he succeeded in pulling it open.

'That's interesting,' he said, 'there's a motor bike parked in front of the fireplace.'

'Looks like they've scarpered,' Misset suggested.

'Go back to sleep,' Pel replied savagely and marched back to the car. 'Did you find Jean-Paul and Mad Max?' he said to Darcy.

'Not yet. Want to try Lorette?'

Outside Mâcon, they pulled up outside her house. The shutters were firmly closed and the vineyard office was locked; the long silent rows of vines were empty. The manager's flat was too.

138

13

Pujol was waiting for them in the corridor chewing his finger ends.

'What have you got apart from a bad habit?' Pel bellowed as he slammed into his office.

'A few gaps,' Pujol replied doubtfully.

'Fire away,' Pel said lighting up. 'Your big bad boss is waiting for his bedtime story.'

Pujol sat, carefully opened his file and took a deep breath. 'On the day of the hold-up at the airport Jacqueline and Willis were not positively identified as present at the party between 14.00 and 16.30. I was told they'd gone for a siesta in their van having drunk too much at midday. Willis reeled off first, Jacqueline followed a little later. Lorette and the manager spent the afternoon in bed and were not seen again until they emerged for dinner at 19.00. François was in Beaune but apart from the barman who spoke to him on the way in and again on his way out of the city, no one remembers him.'

'And Mad Max?'

'There are no gaps in her day, she had a *masseuse, coiffeuse* or consultant with her all the time.'

'Jean-Paul?'

'His feet were seen sticking out from the shade of a tree all afternoon from the other side of the lake, but he was fishing alone.' Pujol paused. 'Burais spoke to him as they left the lunch table at 13.45, and went to see what he'd caught sometime before 17.00.'

'Well, don't stop there,' Pel growled. 'If I know you there's more.'

'With the exception of Mad Max,' Pujol went on, 'and

given that witnesses are rarely one hundred per cent accurate with their timings, all of them could have reached the airport, participated in the hold-up and returned to their original positions during the unaccounted-for hours, but', he added cautiously, 'there's the problem of transport.'

It had been too good to be true.

'Jacqueline and Willis said they were sleeping and weren't seen but their Ban the Bomb van was very much in evidence all the time, it never moved.'

'The motor bike, did they have it with them at the party?'

'It wasn't seen.'

'That doesn't prove it wasn't hidden behind a hedge down the lane.'

'But so far I haven't been able to prove it was,' Pujol pointed out. 'Lorette and the manager arrived in her car; they handed the keys to the receptionist when they checked in to have it moved into the shade. It was, and stayed there until they checked out.'

'Another car waiting for them?'

'I tried all the hire-car companies with no luck,' Pujol said sadly.

'That doesn't mean a thing. Go on.'

'Jean-Paul left his car in an underground garage until the following morning – we already have the proof.'

'Hitch-hiked to the heist?' Pel suggested gloomily. However, it was all they had. He marched Pujol back to the sergeants' room where he found the remains of his team poring over lesser problems.

'Pay attention,' he ordered. 'Bardolle, you're a countryman, get over to the lake where Jean-Paul was fishing, find the tree he was seen to be sleeping under and work out how he could have removed himself, travelled to the airport and returned to the same spot without being seen.'

'I know the lake, Patron,' Bardolle replied heavily. 'It's

140

a very private set-up, only one entrance and nothing but fields all round.'

'With trees and hedges to hide behind,' Pel exploded, 'and you know damn well farmers always go the same way across a field to get to another so they don't damage the crops – look for their tracks, and anyone else's. Take Brochard with you and when you've done that go to the site of the rock and roll concert where Jacqueline and Willis spent the day. You're looking for a place where they could have hidden a motor bike before arriving but within a short walking distance of the property. Aimedieu!'

'Sir!'

'Double check Maxine's story then the hours François spent in Beaune.'

Pujol was sulking behind his boss. 'And me, sir?'

Pel spun round on him. 'You stay here and collate the information that comes in – I can't risk letting you go out.' It was meant to be a compliment but sounded more like a ticking off. 'And while you're waiting you can double check Lorette's little love affair at the Périphérique motel. Well, don't just sit there, get moving!'

Pel didn't expect them to turn up the trump card but he had no choice – someone robbed the plane, why not the Blau family? And they'd all mysteriously disappeared.

An *avis de recherche* had gone out for all of them. With the help of the Préfectures they'd been able to give the registration numbers, makes and colours of the cars driven by the three sisters and their men. Maxine had been quick to respond with a sharp dose of venom into Pel's ear, demanding to know what it was all about. She'd been stopped by a surly policeman and taken to the local gendarmerie in their car like a common criminal. 'And my husband away on a business trip!' she screamed. 'Tell

141

these little upstarts to take me back to my Mercedes immediately.' Pel sighed; at least they knew where she was. However, she didn't know where Jean-Paul had gone, not exactly. 'North,' she snapped, 'and what's so odd about that? He's often away during the week.'

Pel drove slowly home, thinking hard. Perhaps there was nothing odd at all, perhaps he was jumping to conclusions and they'd never find out where the gold had gone to, but there had been too many coincidences – and their alibis had been too precise, every one of them. Innocent people can't usually recall what they were doing on a given day, not immediately; the Blaus had. He slipped through the front door like a thief, hoping Madame Routy wouldn't notice his arrival. Pouring himself a small whisky from the decanter in the sitting-room, he settled himself into his favourite chair with the Gameboy but he was still thinking about the Blaus. Maxine as the cover, to cause disturbance and keep everyone informed of what the police were up to – she was clever enough to organise it all; Jean-Paul, the international businessman with seemingly innocent trips all over the place to set up the inevitable selling; Lorette, a greedy woman with a manager who'd already shown interest in more than her grapes; François, her peasant husband, probably nothing to do with it at all, simply the farmhand; Jacqueline, always poverty stricken and shacked up with the American biker, Willis, who'd been suspected of minor drug smuggling – although Pel had to admit he didn't think either of them was capable of much more; the old boy Blau, death by misadventure, silly old fool forgot to take his pills.

The Gameboy sneered at him. He'd lost, and pressing the buttons on the little grey box he started again in earnest. But it wasn't the only puzzle he'd put together incorrectly.

*

142

The following morning Pel and Darcy were going over their few hard facts when Commissaire Clouet from Avignon rang.

'They're very alike,' he said dismally. 'Both of them enjoy shouting their mouths off, don't they?'

Pel had a good idea who he was talking about but he asked anyway, just to be sure.

'The Blau sisters,' Clouet confirmed. 'We picked up Lorette for you, she was hiding in the country club on the coast here, with', he added, 'a coloured gentleman.'

Pel reached for the Gauloises but Darcy was already helping himself. 'What's her story?' he asked, snatching the packet back and distributing cigarettes over his shoulder.

'She says she was taking a short holiday with a friend after the *vendange*. Do you want to talk to her?'

Pel was retrieving tobacco from the carpet. 'Not bloody likely,' he called. 'Clouet, if necessary tie her up and gag her with anything you can lay your hands on, but you've got to search their room, their belongings and their car, you're looking for gold.'

'Gold?' Clouet repeated, then fell silent.

Pel readjusted his dress and dragged hard on the cigarette that was at last between his lips, emitting clouds of soothing smoke. 'Gold coins,' he explained.

'Pel, I'm coming up to see you,' Clouet announced and rang off abruptly.

'Well,' Pel said, switching the phone off, 'we've got three of them.'

'Four to go, then,' Darcy commented.

'It was four that held up the plane.'

'Four men,' Darcy pointed out.

'Four people,' his boss corrected, 'covered from head to foot so no one could tell whether they were men or women.'

'With all due respect, Patron, even wearing a mechanic's overalls a woman still looks like a woman.'

143

'Not if her head is covered by a balaclava and she's got flat rubber boots on her feet.'

'There are other things that give a woman away; protuberances out front.'

'You haven't met Jacqueline, have you?' Pel replied doubtfully. 'She's a very flat-chested young lady.'

As most people were making their way back to work after the lunch break, Pel contemplated a plastic-covered sandwich and a warm bottle of beer that had been sitting on his desk for over an hour. He'd been checking and rechecking everything. It was possible, he kept telling himself, but not likely – not that that was anything to go on. As he chewed dolefully on the bread and ham, Clouet walked in grinning from ear to ear. It was so out of character with the miserable mask he normally wore that it put Pel right off the idea of eating anything at all.

'You did say gold coins?' Clouet asked, eyeing the half-finished sandwich.

'I did. *Louis d'or.*'

'That's what I thought. Like this one?' he said pleasantly, placing a single unimpressive brass-coloured disc on Pel's desk.

'Where the hell . . .?'

'Are you going to eat that? I haven't had any lunch.'

'Tell me where you got this,' Pel said, turning over the coin, searching for the little details that gave away its value, 'and I'll buy you a proper meal with a bottle of decent wine. Presumably you found it on our loud-mouthed Lorette?'

'So far we've found nothing on her,' Clouet replied. 'However, the manager of the Hôtel Majestic is a conscientious man and doesn't enjoy having people die in his hotel. When the police were involved he enjoyed it even less. He waited until I gave him permission to let the cleaners into Blau's room as instructed. I'd already done my own quick search and found the alphabetulol.'

'Acebutolol,' Pel corrected.

'Yes, quite – anyway, I told him that if anything else was found he was to tell me. I didn't think any more about it thanks to Maxine yelling at me about the autopsies, inefficiency and inconvenience – that one is enough to turn Rambo to jelly. The manager had had another crisis too, strikes in the kitchen or something, but he did bring this in eventually. One of the cleaners picked it up in Blau's room. He saw her bend down to retrieve it and whipped it off her before she could pocket it.'

'Did Maxine see it?'

'No, she was long gone, thank God, but one of my men did. He knows a bit about things like this.' Clouet looked hungrily at Pel's sandwich. 'Well, I told him to find out. Yesterday evening he explained that it may well be part of the hoard of gold that disappeared during the war. While most of it went to Switzerland, some ended up in Portugal, Spain and the Middle East. Did you know that a total of 781 million dollars' worth was taken from ten countries, including fifty-three million from France? Belgium, Holland, Austria, Czechoslovakia were victims too. I can't remember them all but he mentioned Poland, I know. Then we had the panic on with Lorette, and I remembered Blau was Polish, wasn't he? And you asking me to search her for gold coins . . .'

Pel was turning it over in his hand. It didn't look any more valuable than the buttons on the blazer his wife had bought for him in Paris, but he knew it was worth a small fortune. 'Where exactly was it found?' he asked.

'It was in the corner of the room under the curtains.'

Pel stroked his chin thoughtfully and reached for a much-needed cigarette; it would help him think. French gold stolen by the Germans, stolen back by the Polish refugee, Blau, and stolen again from him. Or had it been?

145

Had he stolen it from the Germans, or could he have been paid by them? Perhaps that was why he was so anxious to get rid of it before the international enquiry turned up at his door to accuse him of theft from the French, or worse, being a collaborator with the thieving Germans. Is that why he ran away to Sète at the end of the war, when he should have stayed in Beauzile where he'd been well liked? A traitor to the people he lived amongst? Where then did Mariette come into the mystery? If she didn't, why had he sent the gold back to Burgundy? He'd muttered something about his past catching him up and paying him back. The gold coin was found in his room – had he set up the whole caper to clear his name, sending his ill-gotten gains disguised as perfume? Once it was well clear of him, his home, his factory and his family, he organised the robbery to get his fortune back and to hide it in Burgundy. That would mean his daughters were after all innocent. Or was he really a Polish refugee who'd haphazardly scooped up a bagful of gold from the fleeing Germans' offices as he himself ran for his life and it was his three girls that had been lying through their teeth all along? Was it Jacqueline who had dropped it? Or someone else? Pel's brain ached; all they knew for certain was that Blau was now dead and someone else had the loot.

Clouet's stomach rumbled. 'How about eating?' he said.

14

While they were finishing their meal across the road at the Bar Transvaal, Darcy joined them and ordered coffee. He reached over and pinched the inevitable cigarette.

'Have you given up buying them?' Pel barked.

'No, I'm helping you cut down on your consumption,' he replied smoothly, dazzling them with his Disney smile. 'Every one I smoke is one less for you. They've found the cars,' he added casually.

Once the information had penetrated, Pel slammed his knife and fork down. 'Well, go on,' he growled. 'Where?'

'Reims,' Darcy said. 'A white Renault Nevada estate and Jean-Paul's blue metallic Mercedes. They'd been parked on opposite sides of the town in spaces reserved for the occupants of two large blocks of flats. The flats are being searched for the drivers at the moment.'

'They won't find them,' Pel retorted.

'That's what I thought,' Darcy agreed, 'but it had to be done.'

'There's a clever mind behind all this. Both Jacqueline and Jean-Paul stop in Reims, they must be working together,' Pel said thoughtfully, 'but if they'd stopped to do a deal in Reims they'd have hidden their cars. Are there any numismatists there?'

'No one registered with the Syndicat National des Experts.'

'So they're not selling yet if they've got the gold, they don't know we're after them, but they've covered the possibility on the off-chance. Perhaps the rest of the family are after them, and this is a diversion. My guess is that they've simply changed cars again, and now we don't know what they're driving. This is a bloody well organised scheme.'

'Pel, excuse me for interfering,' Clouet said, delicately wiping his mouth, 'but Reims is famous for champagne, perhaps they simply stopped to celebrate.'

'Perhaps they're in the middle of a passionate love affair and are being careful not to be caught by Mad Max, although I doubt it,' Pel added gloomily.

'Reims is north of Paris,' Clouet went on, 'and well past Strasbourg, the obvious places to sell the treasure.'

'So where the hell are they headed?'

'There's not much beyond Reims except Belgium or La Manche.'

'A Frenchman in his right mind wouldn't do business with a Belgian.'

'So that leaves the English Channel,' Clouet said innocently. 'Boulogne or Calais, take your pick, London's just a short hop from either.'

Pel leant forward over the table, sending the arriving coffee cascading on to Clouet's shirt. 'Alert both ports,' he said urgently to Darcy. 'Fax all necessary information. We've got to stop them before they leave the country. Get two teams ready to leave – you're going to Boulogne with one lot, I'll take the other to Calais. Get going!'

As Darcy disappeared, Pel turned to mop up Clouet's sticky front. 'Fancy a day at the seaside?' he asked.

Ten minutes after the two helicopters had lifted off and headed north, Pujol, who'd been left behind, was trying to talk to Pel. It wasn't an easy conversation over the noise of the rotating blades but with a good deal of shouting he understood what Pujol was trying to communicate.

'I've cracked the locked door problem!'

'You were supposed to be cracking Lorette's motel story!'

'I'm doing that too, but the Majestic called, I thought you'd like to know. Blau could have been murdered after all!'

'Prove it.'

'Affirmative! Manager says Jacqueline carried handbag into room when they found body. She dropped it by bed, he thought it was shock. Not sure now. He says that she steadied herself with hand on bedside table to retrieve bag. He heard something clink on surface, key to room, it hadn't been there before, table empty on arrival. She put it there after he'd opened door with master key. Patron! She could have pushed acebutolol under bed at the same time!'

Pel was momentarily silent. And the gold coin had rolled out of her bag – had she stolen it from her dying father, or from the plane? Both ways she was as guilty as hell of something.

'Only an idea, sir!'

'If she confesses, I'll buy you a drink!'

'What, Patron? Can't hear you!'

'Switch the little bugger off,' Pel said to de Troq' who was sitting beside him.

The English Channel came into sight, a vast dark mass churning in the roaring wind. As they stepped out on to the concrete helipad they felt its full force; it stood their hair on end and flung their unbuttoned jackets open, making the four policemen look like fledgelings preparing for their first flight. Pel, de Troq', Annie and Cheriff crossed to a low building and were relieved to close the door on the grim coastal weather. Within minutes a car had arrived to take them to the Port Authority's headquarters where Pel made his request to the ferry-boat companies.

A boat was due in from Dover in an hour; it would change crew, embark the already arriving vehicles and leave an hour later. Each car would have to have a ticket verified, proof of which would be the bright orange sticker added to the windscreen. It would be de Troq' and Annie in the appropriate uniform who would do this, discreetly looking into each car for a face they recognised, while Cheriff checked the foot passengers through the main building. There had been an initial protest that this would cause delays but finally it was agreed; the men and women normally on duty were told that trainee personnel were being put through their paces and that they were to watch and answer questions only. The police were issued with the company's stock of mobile telephones, even Pel, who was to sit in the watch tower up above them all. A very patient young woman explained four times how to make it work but he was still baffled and hoped he wouldn't have to use it.

The Adjutant Chef from the local gendarmerie arrived and agreed immediately to install his men around the perimeter of the docks. It was the first bit of action he'd had that year and he was delighted to be involved. Pel quietly hoped he'd be able to keep him under control if it came to it.

And finally the group of special police arrived, six highly trained slim youngsters, their commanding officer looking no more than an overgrown adolescent; however, through the open door of their van Pel caught a glimpse of the black hoods of his men and their horrifying armoury. To his surprise the commander was quietly respectful, listening to their account of the situation and agreeing with the decisions taken: they were to stay out of sight until they were needed, if they were needed.

150

Saluting, he turned back towards their van; within thirty seconds the van had been hidden and the men had disappeared. Pel lit up. Holy Mother of God, he was thinking, let it be peaceful. He hated confrontations with loaded guns, someone always got hurt, often one of his men.

In Boulogne, Clouet and Darcy organised a similar arrangement and, satisfied that everything was in order, Clouet picked up his mobile phone and tapped out the appropriate number for Calais.

Pel stared in horror as his phone beeped and flashed at his elbow. He snatched it up and pressed a number of buttons, smiling in embarrassment at the young woman as she got up from her desk to rescue him. With luck Pel finally did the right thing and heard Clouet's frustration.

'Blasted modern gadgets,' he was saying. 'Here, Darcy, you see if you can get the thing to work.'

'All present and correct in Boulogne, Patron,' Darcy said confidently.

'Here too,' Pel confirmed, amazed by the magic of modern technology.

'All we have to do now is wait.'

'As always. If they don't show up for this one we'll change docks and wait for the next departure with a different cross-Channel ferry company.'

'At least you're out of the wind – I've got to go and suffer outside with Nosjean. They're ready to start embarkation here, the ship's due to leave in half an hour – that is, if the queue of foot passengers ever gets past Misset.'

'Why have you got Misset with you? The man's an idiot.'

'He was available when the flag went up.'

'Keep me informed.'

Pel put the phone down carefully and five minutes later the kind young woman came over to suggest that he cut

151

the communication by pressing the button marked *'ligne'*. 'Otherwise,' she explained, 'no one else can call you or Monsieur on the other end.' It was enough to make a man worry rats.

The ship in Boulogne slowly loaded its cargo of vehicles and passengers, while in Calais the boat from Dover docked, emptying its contents on to the quayside. Pel was rapidly becoming impatient but eventually he saw de Troq' and Annie methodically making their way between the waiting vehicles looking at tickets and slapping the large orange dots on to the windscreens. Half an hour later the order was given to start loading and the neatly parked rows of cars slowly disappeared into the guts of the ship. Cheriff called to say he'd finished checking the foot passengers and the burly men waiting beside the walls of the ship prepared to cast off the massive cables holding the huge vessel steady in its dock. As it slipped over the horizon, Pel's disappointment was doubled by Clouet's message of nothing to report from Boulogne.

For a couple of hours they relaxed before changing places into another company's offices and uniforms to prepare for the next sailing. Sitting out of sight with his telephone ready to frighten the life out of him, Pel considered the situation. For once he was glad he was a policeman; he was bored to tears watching the migration of late holiday-makers and businessmen, uninterested in the swooping, crying seagulls and less than amused by the weather that raged around him. If he'd had to do it day after day for a living, he would have given up and gone home long ago. Chasing criminals all these years hadn't been such a bad life after all.

Another ship arrived and through the smoke of thousands of cigarettes he watched the cars come out and make their way to the exit. De Troq' and Annie appeared again and started their damp trip down the waiting queues. It all went like clockwork; night was falling fast and there were fewer vehicles to be loaded but every one was checked. For the second time Pel saw a ferry slip its lines and leave France. Darcy still had nothing to report.

But Pujol did.

His highly excited voice rang into Pel's ears. 'Bardolle and Brochard think they've found where Willis hid his bike. I've got the experts out to the site to try and find the evidence. He could have collected Jean-Paul from a small lane not far from his lake,' he added, 'but that's only guesswork, Burais said he was asleep under a tree – he swears blind his boots didn't move all afternoon.'

'And Lorette?' Pel insisted.

'Haven't cracked that one yet.'

'Then hurry up!'

If Jacqueline and Willis had feigned drunkenness and slipped off to a hidden motor bike, one of them could have collected Jean-Paul and taken him to the robbery. But what about the rest of them? If Jacqueline and Willis had the bike hidden, Lorette and the manager could have had a second car parked somewhere, climbed through the window of the motel and made the quick dash to a rendezvous with Jean-Paul, Jacqueline and Willis. But that made five, and there'd only been four on the runway. Perhaps Jean-Paul had nothing to do with it – after all, his boots hadn't moved all afternoon. If his feet were in the boots, of course.

Going back to their original positions, they sorted themselves out for the last departure that evening, the midnight ferry; after that they could turn in for the night before starting all over again at dawn the following morning. Pel was wondering whether their rush for the coast had been a mistake but he had to sit it out for

153

another twelve hours; he couldn't think of anywhere else the gold could be headed for if that was what they were up to.

It was mostly lorries being checked and loaded at eleven thirty, only a few British cars were waiting to go aboard. Their tickets were quickly seen to be in order before they were sent through for embarkation. It looked as if the ship would leave a few minutes early when two headlights came very quickly across Calais's vast and empty waiting area.

15

In Boulogne Clouet and Darcy were watching Nosjean at Ticket Control. He gave the signal but the driver in the waiting car had done the trip before and noticed immediately that the orange sticker had been put on the wrong side. He accelerated away fast, tried to turn and, skidding violently on the oily tarmac, came to a sudden halt with a bollard well and truly embedded in his bonnet. He sprang from the car and ran hell for leather for the open mouth of the ship, a second man tearing after him. Darcy and Nosjean gave chase, stumbling up the winding stairs, running through the narrow corridors and shoving lethargic families crashing into their cabins.

A large group of rugby supporters were arguing about which bar was the most convivial for getting drunk in when Jean-Paul and François collided with them. While they were trying to force their way through, the two detectives dived for their ankles in a spectacular tackle. The whole lot collapsed and for three minutes it was a free for all before Clouet arrived with a loudspeaker and brought the scrum to a halt. There were a number of black eyes and wrenched shoulders but in the end the rugby men struggled to their feet and, slapping everyone on the back, limped off happily towards some serious inebriation. Panting for breath, Darcy and Nosjean formally arrested Jean-Paul and François while Clouet shook hands with the captain. The gathering groups of onlookers applauded enthusiastically.

*

In the watch tower in Calais, Pel picked up his phone and started punching buttons. Nothing happened until he remembered the essential one marked *'ligne'* and he started all over again.

'Stand by,' he said calmly to the local police. In the night-watchmen's wooden huts beyond the dock's gates, the gendarmes stubbed out their cigarettes furiously and swigged back the remaining coffee. In the main building, stuffed into a small office behind the canteen, the special police checked their arms and ammunition.

Pel closed the communication and watched. De Troq' waved the large dark car to a halt, spoke to the driver, examined the ticket offered, removed the section covering the Calais–Dover crossing and went round to the passenger's side to slap the sticker on to the windscreen.

All the other cars had received their dot on the driver's side.

De Troq' took a few steps back into his shelter, having told the waiting car they'd be called aboard any moment now. Annie went in immediately after him. 'Yes?' she asked quietly.

De Troq' turned his back to the car. 'If it is, they've both cut their hair and taken a bath. You have a look.'

Annie went back out, looked into the car and smiled. 'Good evening,' she said. 'We'll have you on board in a minute.' She walked off towards the buildings, lifting her mobile phone out of her breast pocket as she went. 'That's it,' she announced brightly. 'Pretty sure it's the last car for this sailing. Let's shut up shop.'

It was almost normal procedure, but the waiting police knew what she meant: once the exits were closed and the ship shut tight, they'd move in. The woman in the car was feeling nervous; she looked round as if searching for something. Above them was the well-lit watch tower. There was someone staring down at them puffing hard on a cigarette – she couldn't see his face. The man who'd checked their tickets was leaning against the glass wall of his shelter waiting for instructions; his female colleague was almost at the door of the main building. Then she turned in her seat and saw the uniformed police walking away from the locked entrance.

'Get out of here, John,' she hissed. 'Something's up.'

Willis put the car in gear and shot off with his tyres squealing. Pel shouted orders as he saw the car turn in terrible shrieking circles. There was nowhere for them to go. He saw de Troq' and Annie running for the ship; they'd realised the only way out was over the water. The drawbridge was slowly being winched back and they had to leap across a gaping hole of churning waves. Willis had made the same discovery; wherever he turned the car he was faced by solid gates or a dive into the sea. He wrenched on the wheel and, as the ferry-boat employees scattered from his path, he shot off the still retreating drawbridge, his engine howling in mid-air, and landed with a resounding bang in the car bay of the boat.

Inside there were still a number of passengers dawdling over the items they needed for the crossing, collecting rugs and pillows and babies' pushchairs. A child was crying with tiredness while his parents argued. De Troq' and Annie crouched on either side of the echoing cavity, hoping to hell Willis and Jacqueline weren't armed. Gunshot in such a confined space would be lethal, the bullets ricocheting in all directions off the thick metal walls.

Cheriff ran from the office where he'd been sorting through the last of the foot passengers and, climbing frantically through a crowd of rucksacks and ambling bodies, he struggled up the gangplank pushing sleepy people out of his way. He had a problem finding the right staircase, the inside of the ship was like a maze, but at last he alighted outside one of the heavy iron doors of the car bay to hear the internal communication system jingle into action. Pel announced clearly that the boat was about

157

to sail and would those still with their vehicles please hurry upstairs. There was a shuffle of activity as the stragglers made an effort to get to the doors. What Pel wanted was the general public out, Jacqueline and Willis still in and all the huge impenetrable doors of the cargo hold shut, but Willis wasn't willing to be trapped so simply.

He leapt from the car, a shotgun in his hands. 'Nobody move,' he yelled and shot wildly at the still open tailgate. The echoing explosion was followed by screams of terror but the bullet disappeared harmlessly into the night.

'Jackie, grab the kid that's crying,' Willis ordered.

Having savagely slapped the mother, she roughly dragged a sobbing overtired child towards their car and pushed him in.

De Troq' stood up. 'I'm a police officer,' he said clearly. 'Release the child. I'll take his place.'

'No way!'

'I'm worth more to you than a child.'

'*Flics* know how to cheat, I'll keep the kid, you wouldn't dare let me hurt him. Tell your bosses to let me out of here, to open the dock gate and let me go. I'm taking the kid with me. I'll stop and let him out an hour from here, if I'm not followed. If I am, I'll push him out at top speed and you can scrape him off the road.'

The mother stifled a pitiful wail as her husband held her back.

Pel ordered the floodlights outside to be extinguished as he called the special police into play. The situation was exactly what they dreaded, a child hostage. A child that might panic held by a desperate man with a gun.

So far the general public upstairs knew nothing and that was the way they wanted to keep it. The ship's officers had been told two stowaways were hiding in the car bay and all access was to be denied. Pel made his way down, checking security, certain the hell-hole was

158

sealed off. Stopping briefly to tread on a half-smoked Gauloise he stepped out into the hold. He called to Willis, his voice sounding hollow in the half-empty belly of the ship: 'I'm Chief Inspector Pel. Release the child and we'll talk.'

'No talking, I've told you what I want, get on with it!'

Jacqueline was leaning against the car door looking horribly pleased with herself. Willis stood in front of it, erect and proudly holding his rifle. 'Start organising it, or I start shooting,' he shouted, and to prove his point he let off another bullet. It bounced off the walls, zipping back and forth, but mercifully hit no one. Willis frowned.

'He hasn't thought this through,' Pel whispered to Cheriff standing behind him. 'He's no professional and that makes it even more dangerous. He's totally unpredictable.'

'I don't see much action!' Willis yelled again, pointing the barrel of his gun at the floor in front of the terrified huddle of trapped passengers. He pulled the trigger. The bullet hit the deck with a twang and lifted back off. An elderly man cried out, staggered and fell. A red stain oozed sickeningly through his pale woollen sweater.

The child inside the car was fascinated. Suddenly no longer tired or crying he was sitting up watching the proceedings. People were shouting at each other. He looked up towards the mirror and caught a glimpse of two black shadows peeling off from the night outside and sliding silently behind the pillars at the far end. He turned and stared hard but there was no one – he must have imagined it. He turned back again, it was more interesting in front. Then he saw the keys. They'd left them in the ignition. A forbidden toy, he knew he should never touch them, but he just had to – he turned the key the way he'd seen mum and dad do it . . .

The car bounced forward.

Willis was knocked clean off his feet. The gun exploded

again as he was catapulted off the bonnet. A caravan window shattered; glass tinkled on to the metal deck. The car stalled, and Jacqueline sprang to recover the gun. Annie fell on her. De Troq' threw himself across the boot of the car alongside and landed hard on the winded Willis. Pel ambled over with Cheriff, who was already preparing the plastic handcuffs for their prisoners.

The two special policemen clad in black strolled towards the scene nodding in approval. Then Annie opened the car door.

'Sorry,' the boy said with tears in his eyes. 'I didn't mean to.'

Pel pulled his phone from his pocket and gave the all-clear. Suddenly the yawning cavity of the ship was filled with port officials, gendarmes, dockhands, cleaners, odd job men, the lot. He wondered where the hell they'd all come from. Only the special police were missing – they'd arrived, participated and vanished again. Above the sobbing and laughter a siren was heard as an ambulance sped over the tarmac for the wounded and shocked. The elderly man who'd been shot had been lucky, the bullet had only sliced through the side of his beer paunch; he'd bled copiously but was in no danger.

At last the ship sailed with corks popping. The captain, never one to miss an opportunity, had ordered free champagne for his passengers.

In the small hours of the following morning the prisoners were locked safely behind bars in the two ports to await their trip back to Burgundy. The two cars were collected and left before the prisoners, and Pel was reluctantly still attached to his mobile phone. 'Damn thing,' he said to Darcy. 'I could get used to it if I tried hard.'

160

'Well done, Patron. See you back in the office,' Darcy replied and the line went dead.

'To get the proof down on paper,' Pel muttered. 'Hell's teeth, it'll take years to sort out – I still don't know how they did it.'

16

Leguyder was ecstatic, he'd never seen so much gold. It had been hidden in small pouches hanging from the springs inside the seats of the two cars.

Pel was less ecstatic, but with the help of Pujol and Debray's computer calculations, he was beginning to understand the puzzle. Except for Lorette and the manager – he couldn't fit them in anywhere. And of course Maxine, the brains – they had no proof she was involved at all, although he expected at least one of their prisoners to point the finger at her. It would have to be enough.

He'd allowed the four prisoners to cross paths in the corridors but not to speak. Each one knew the others were there but not what they were saying to the police. By the end of the day they'd all be accusing each other, he hoped.

He lit a cigarette, gathered his papers together, and called to Darcy to accompany him to the interview room. Jean-Paul was to be the first candidate.

It wasn't the same self-confident smooth businessman who now sat with his head in his hands. For a start he was unshaven and his smart designer suit looked as if it had been slept in. It had.

He gratefully accepted a Gauloise. 'Thank you,' he said sadly. 'I prefer King Edwards, but I suppose I'm going to have to get used to these now.' He fell silent, studying the smoke rise, not wanting to answer Pel's questions. He was asked one last time to make a statement. And then he slowly unravelled his story. Old Monsieur Blau had once talked about his hidden treasure. Jean-Paul and Maxine had discussed it during the early days of their marriage but it was forgotten until she came into the office one day

162

and told him she'd caught her father playing with gold coins.

'It was around the time that the perfume samples were being prepared for shipment,' he said sadly, 'and he'd insisted on Burgundy as their destination. I had a brainwave when I remembered the inscription I'd seen in two of his books. Christ, I thought, he couldn't be daft enough to want to send the perfume to Mariette. Then I put two and two together, it added up to millions. It wasn't too difficult to find where he'd hidden the treasure at the château – behind his books, like the booze.'

'Why didn't you take it from him then?' Pel asked.

'Because he'd have known immediately that it was me and reported it to the police. Questions would have been asked and his whole sordid past would have come out. He didn't give a fig about it any more, it even amused him that Maxine was terrified of public humiliation.' He looked up at Pel with a beaten expression. 'You may find this hard to believe but while I hated the old scoundrel, I do love my wife, I couldn't have risked putting her through that. Do you know, when she found out for sure that it was the gold that had been stolen she was relieved. At last, she said, we can turn the page on my father's history and close the book.'

'But she was the one who organised it,' Pel said, frowning.

'She had nothing to do with it. I wanted to get it back for her, for us – she didn't know what we'd planned.'

Pel was still not convinced.

Jean-Paul gazed at him for a moment, then he shrugged. 'Anyway, having found the treasure neatly packed into pouches, I watched him carefully. It was obvious what he was up to. Sending back what he'd taken to the woman he'd been obsessed with ever since he'd run away from Beauzile. It was pathetic. I almost laughed when I thought of him wanting to reimburse his tart.

163

'I sent François to find out where she was but it was useless, no one in the village had ever heard of Mariette, so we decided the gold had to be taken before it reached her.'

'And Mariline Philibert?'

'Is a student researching the Second World War, pestering old men and asking silly questions. We found out about her, and François went to see her, but she came to the same dead end with the old priest.'

'She nearly came to a dead end in a car crash,' Pel said. 'Who pierced the rubber pipe?'

'What rubber pipe?'

'Behind the wheel – it drained the car of brake fluid.'

'I really don't know what you're talking about. The closest I ever get to fiddling with a car is changing gears.'

Pel was inclined to believe him. 'Go on,' he said.

'I'm a failed dermatologist, but thanks to my wife I'm a successful businessman. I wanted to prove to her that I'd been worth the investment, get back her inheritance for her. It wasn't fair she was being excluded. And François was all for it, he couldn't wait to wave two fingers at that bitch Lorette and piss off to sunny Spain with his latest bit of fluff. Trouble was, he's not frightfully intelligent when it comes to working things out. We needed someone else to come in with us. He suggested Jacqueline, she's an old flame of his. It seemed stupid at the time, but after thinking about it a while I realised she was perfect. She was bitter about being continually poor – she always blamed Blau for that. Mind you, he never gave anything away free to Maxine or Lorette. Only trouble was, she wanted Willis in. I finally agreed when she pointed out he spoke perfect English, albeit with a strong American accent, and that would have been to our advantage when selling the gold in London. No one thinks twice about our transatlantic cousins having hoards of money.'

Pel offered him another cigarette. 'And Blau's death?'

164

'A nasty mistake. Jacqueline should have been more careful. But we agreed that it was to our advantage – with him out of the way the chances were that no one would ever find out what had been stolen and we were in the clear to deal.'

'To sell the ill-gotten gains of a Polish refugee on the run,' Pel added.

Jeal-Paul stared at him but said nothing.

'So tell me about your trip from the lake to the airport.'

The prisoner blinked several times, realising he'd said far too much. 'I've just lost my memory,' he said slowly, 'and I deny everything I've said. I refuse to answer another question until I've seen my lawyer. If you can't prove I was there you can only charge me with possession of stolen goods – and I didn't even know they were there, I was innocently taking François on holiday, it must've been him.' He shut his mouth tight and didn't say another word.

At first François was confused by what had happened and ignored the questions Darcy asked.

'It's all a big mistake,' he muttered, shaking his head. 'We shouldn't have been caught. When your boss came to see me at the vineyard office,' he explained, 'I thought we'd slipped up somewhere, but it was only about Mariline – that was a relief, I can tell you. Nice girl, rotten about the car crash. Did you catch the man who did it?'

'No, we didn't,' Darcy said, 'and you didn't catch much skirt in Beaune on the afternoon of the robbery, did you?'

'Skirt? Everyone thinks that's all I do, but you're wrong,' he cried, 'I wasn't chasing skirt, I was making a name for myself.'

'One that'll go down in the history of crime.'

'It's better than being Lorette's peasant all my life.'

'I'm surprised she let you in on the hold-up.'

'She wouldn't have if she'd known, but she was so busy stroking her little black lap-dog she didn't even suspect I was planning to remove her inheritance from under her upturned nose.'

'It must have taken a lot of planning,' Darcy prompted.

'It did,' François said proudly, 'complicated too, but it went off without a hitch. Absolutely perfect.'

'I don't suppose you had much to do, then?'

That's when the whole story came tumbling out. François told them everything, like a small child pouring out the details of his latest adventure.

Jean-Paul had done the planning, not Maxine. He'd left his car in the underground car-park and was picked up by a colleague and taken to the lake. Jacqueline made an exhibition of herself at the party – 'She's good at that,' François said, grinning smugly – 'while Willis collected the bike and shot off to our rendezvous at the service station where I was waiting. We whipped the first car, I'd been watching it for months, and we took it and the bike back to the service station, then we went for the other car, I'd watched that one too. You see, it all came down to me being efficient.'

'Go on,' Darcy said.

'We got that one back to the service station and, making sure my car and the bike were well parked in amongst the other hundreds, he went off to pick Jean-Paul up from the lane not far from the lake and I went to get Jacqueline. Jean-Paul had set up his boots under a tree by his fishing rods and Jacqueline had crawled off to sleep in the van. Clever wasn't it?'

Darcy nodded but said nothing.

'And off we went to the airport, cut the lock on the service gate and when the plane came down in we went.'

Darcy lit a cigarette and handed François one. It was pathetic to see the glee with which he recounted the story.

'Back to the service station with the gold, and divided

it up into saddlebags and fishing baskets, one each, see, changed back to my car and the bike and off we went. I took Jean-Paul back. He only just made it, a bloke turned up to talk to him as he was removing his boots from under the tree, said something about him not catching much. If only he'd known what we'd caught! Not a few little tiddlers, the big one! After that, well, I went for a drink, Willis and Jacqueline went back to the party and retrieved the bike the next morning, put it in the van on their way out. Brilliant, don't you think?'

'Except that you got caught,' Darcy pointed out, extinguishing his cigarette and François's joy.

Willis, who had been the most vicious at the end, said little and what he did say didn't help – he demanded to see the Ambassador of the United States of America. Pel left him to stew a while longer and went to see Jacqueline.

She was spitting venom, screaming about how she'd always been cheated by her sisters and her father – yes, Jean-Paul was the brains but she was the one who'd persuaded the wets they could really pull it off.

'When it came to it,' she shouted, 'they lost their nerve, started whingeing about wanting to call it off. I was the one with the guts.'

'Guts enough to kill your own father?' Pel asked charmingly.

'I didn't kill him, it was a heart attack.'

'A heart attack induced by the interruption of his treatment.'

'He had his acebutolol with him the whole time – if he didn't take them that was his fault,' she snapped. 'I expect he dropped them under the bed. If the police had looked hard enough they'd have found them.'

That was enough for Pel. It had taken him weeks of practice to say the name correctly, and she hadn't even hesitated. All she had to do was look at the notice inside the cardboard box to find out what effect it would have if a patient was denied his prescribed dose. She'd obviously found it compulsive reading. And she'd known exactly where the drugs had been.

'No,' he said confidently, 'you pushed them under the bed when you dropped your handbag, at the same time as you placed the key to his room on the bedside table. Why did you keep the key so long? To make sure he was absolutely dead before you called the manager in to make the discovery?'

Much to Pel's surprise, Jacqueline burst into tears.

'He wanted to see you,' she sobbed, 'that's why he asked me to drive him north. I couldn't let him tell you what had been stolen, we were in the clear with millions' worth of gold to sell. He thought it was Maxine.'

Pel had to admit he had too.

So at least they'd solved the airport hold-up and recovered the gold. Now they knew the truth nearly everything fell into place.

The proof was gathered by Forensics and presented proudly and at length on paper to Pel by a smirking Leguyder. It was one good point to add to their statistics. They still had a few questions they wanted answering, like who the hell was Mariette? What did Mariline have to do with it, if anything? And who stuck a darning needle in the little rubber pipe behind the wheel of her car? And Pel still found it hard to believe Maxine and Lorette had nothing to do with the robbery, but that was that, and they had another thousand or so cases to clear up and keep them busy well into the next year.

But it wasn't over yet.

*

After shouting at the morning meeting that there was to be no slacking, Pel happily sauntered back down the corridor. He'd congratulated Pujol on his extraordinary imagination and nearly frightened the life out of him. It was almost worth a smile, if no one was looking.

Darcy made him jump, coming up behind as he paused to open his office door.

'You need warning lights or a siren fitted,' Pel snarled, 'creeping up on me like that. What is it?'

'Thought you might like to see this,' his second-in-command said, handing over a newspaper.

Pel looked at the obituary of the retired priest at Beauzile. ' . . . died in his sleep after a lifetime devoted to his church and community,' he read, searching for the packet of Gauloises that should have been on his desk.

'The funeral's today, Patron,' Darcy pointed out, lighting up and handing over the cigarettes.

The whole village had turned out to see the *curé* off, and there was a considerable amount of weeping and wailing from the women as the coffin was lowered into the massive marble tomb. Madame Latour and her son were there, dressed in the same clothes as for Blau's funeral, except that they'd added threadbare overcoats. The son was still ill at ease in his stiff suit, the old lady dignified and strangely elegant beneath her wide black hat.

'I would be honoured if you would join me at my house for a drink when it's all over,' she said quietly to Pel.

The house was large and well kept, the shutters newly painted, and despite the fallen leaves the garden looked cared for. Inside, however, it was plain and bare. A miserable fire flickered at the back of a vast fireplace that swallowed what little heat the two logs offered. Madame Latour sat carefully on an old sofa covered with a clean but fraying rug, while her son went into the small kitchen beyond to fetch the glasses and a bottle of eau-de-vie.

'A little drop to warm us up,' she suggested, watching her middle-aged son pour out the clear liqueur. As she took her glass, she toasted the end of an era, and the beginning of another.

'You see, I have a story to tell you, Monsieur Pel. I wish to claim the gold you recovered – it was for me.'

Pel raised his eyebrows. 'But madame, you told me you had never been the mistress of Monsieur Blau.'

'I told you I had never been the mistress of the Polish refugee and that is the truth. He was called Nowak, which was changed to Blau, and was taken in for questioning by the Germans. He died in custody.'

Pel started to say something, but Madame Latour gently raised her hand and continued. 'A young German officer, Erich von Weissenhoff, was told to dispose of the body. He carried it down to the boiler room where they melted down stolen treasure to make it easier for transportation. There he burnt the body of Nowak-Blau, but he kept his papers. You see, the refugee was the same age as the German officer and it occurred to him that this might be his chance to escape from a defeated army. He had become disenchanted with the Reich and, though he feared returning to his homeland possibly to be court-martialled or shot, he feared staying in victorious France more. The Resistance were badly wanting to cut a few German throats. When they finally left us, they left in a hurry, and Erich von Weissenhoff jumped from the convoy saying he had one last score to settle. I'd told him of the Maquis's plan to ambush the Germans, and he came to hide in my loft while his compatriots were surrounded and dealt with. Erich was presumed dead, but he stayed with me for many weeks while the war came to its end, then he set off south as Josephe Blau.

'If the people of my village had discovered him, he would have been murdered. My brother, the priest we buried today, wanted him dead more than anyone – he knew about us, you see – but vowed his silence to save me from being tarred and feathered. The French were not kind to the girls who went with the Germans...' She sighed and delicately took another sip at her glass. 'But believe me, there were good ones: those who were simply men a long way from home, desperately lonely, forced to follow orders, hating the war for disallowing normal compassion and humanity. Erich was one and we had the misfortune to fall in love. In return for my brother's silence I was never to accept another centime from my handsome German. I handed over the two pouches of gold he'd left me and continued to do so every time a money order arrived. With sadness in my heart for my poverty, I watched while the village and its priest flourished from Erich's success as a businessman.'

So Nowak's name was changed to Blau, and von Weissenhoff stole his identity and fled. No wonder the family clammed up when Pel mentioned the Polish refugee.

'But where did the gold come from?' he asked, cautiously tasting the eau-de-vie.

'It was gold the Germans had amassed – there was so much waiting to be melted down they became less careful. Erich took a handful of coins every time he went down to the boiler room, he put it into the pouches I made and we hid them here in this house.'

She picked up her glass again and touched it to her lips. 'So that is my story, *cher* Monsieur Pel, which you have been searching for. Now that Erich and my pious brother are both gone, I can see no point in remaining silent any longer. I am not ashamed of what I did, in fact I'm proud I recognised a gentleman who needed love in the holocaust we endured. I don't have very long before death will finally claim me, and my son, the son of the Baron Erich Wolfgang von Weissenhoff, declared legally in Munich by his father shortly after his birth, now a baron himself, needs his inheritance. We have been alone and poor too long. Erich did what he could, but my brother took it away from us and we've had to work hard to survive. The time has come for my son to have what his father intended for him: the gold should have been delivered to the bank to wait for the day we could use it. I would like you to advise me as to how I should make my claim.'

Pel looked at the tall thin man sitting silently beside his mother; he was nothing more or less than a diffident peasant, but a peasant with a surprising title. He wasn't sure how the courts would deal with Madame Latour's claim on the gold – she'd need a good lawyer – but the baron's son would get something, even if it was only a large slice of the Blau estate: he was after all the only 'living issue of the deceased', the only biological child Blau had, as the three girls were his daughters by adoption. Pel remembered saying, when de Troq' had made the discovery, So what difference does that make? Now he knew. He wanted to laugh, thinking about the hysterical Blau sisters filled with snobbery and greed – he would have loved to be there when they found out they had a brother to share everything with.

He smiled most of the way home, until Mariette's explanation for her silence hit him right between the eyes. It was a good reason for attempted murder.

17

At the Hôtel de Police he stopped and picked up the only senior officer of his team still at his desk. With de Troq' listening, fascinated, they headed down the motorway.

In the fading light, they found Maxine at the end of the jetty, just as they'd found her father. She was shivering under her fur coat, staring out over the water and watching the beginning of a magnificent sunset. To one side of her was a bottle of her father's cognac, to the other a packet of menthol cigarettes. She turned and looked at them with desolate eyes.

'All my life', she said miserably, 'I've tried to keep the family together, honourable and proud. Now look at us; my husband and sister are in jail, my other sister, Lorette, is openly cavorting with a . . .' Words failed her.

'A negro?' Pel suggested.

'Yes,' she said her eyes empty, 'and father is dead, *so sei es.*'

'Was it your father who taught you to speak German?'

'I don't suppose there's any point in denying it now, is there?' she asked, taking the bottle and swigging at the cognac. 'Our shame is complete. Even that great secret is out. Yes, he was a German officer in occupied France.'

'That's history now, madame.'

'You don't understand,' she cried. 'For me to discover my father was a German? There are plenty of Frenchmen who still call them Boche and spit after saying it. We've one or two at the factory. It would have been a disaster socially and for the sales figures of the company a *véritable catastrophe.*' She turned away from the policemen, looking back out over the water. 'When I was little,' she said quietly, 'I believed the stories he told me of his daring escape and good fortune, just as I believed in fairy stories. And he made me love him, he was a good man. But the night before my wedding he told me the truth and tried to convince me that all he had was due to honest hard work. It was too late to suddenly turn my happy childhood into hatred, I adored the old bastard, but I felt deceived, and frightened when he begged me to keep his secret safe for the sake of our inheritance.'

'Painful memories and the past,' Pel said sadly. 'I think you should be worrying more about your future. It is very much in question at the moment. Killing people is illegal, even when it's unintentional.'

'I had nothing to do with his death.'

'And Mariline Philibert?'

'She didn't die.'

'Five innocent people did, madame.'

'I had to stop her. Jean-Paul told me about her, she was researching the lives of refugees who'd stayed in France. Can you imagine if she'd managed to find the real Nowak-Blau family in Poland and tried to reunite them with my father, the man who'd fed the refugee's body into the furnace? I couldn't let her carry on, and I couldn't tell her why she must stop.'

'Madame, I am under the obligation to arrest you for attempted murder, resulting in loss of life to other parties,' Pel announced solemnly. 'Do your stuff, will you?' he said to de Troq'. 'Tell her her rights, all nice and legal so there are no slip-ups.'

As all the reports were being finished, Pel's senior officers gathered round his desk to compare notes. When they'd finally completed their discussion, Darcy asked the question everyone wanted the answer to.

'So how much was the gold worth, Patron?'

'Thirty-two million,' de Troq' replied, 'five hundred and ten thousand francs, give or take a franc or two.'

'That'll keep the new Baron von Weissenhoff in hand-made gumboots and overalls for the rest of his life.'

'I doubt that he'll get any of it, and if he does it won't be for years. I can see the scandal of Nazi gold going on into the next century.'

'But he'll have a small fortune from Blau's declared estate.'

'Once they've sorted out that clause about the "living issue of the deceased".'

'He's sporting a monocle now, has a bit of difficulty keeping it in place, but he's persevering.'

'Good bloody luck to him.'

'I find it all very curious,' Nosjean said quietly, 'and somewhat paradoxical.'

'Those are long words for you,' Pel replied seriously. 'Don't forget we are here to catch criminals – leave the philosophy to more astute men.' He passed a hand over his balding head; it had been a tiring year. 'Now sod off, all of you,' he finally bellowed, 'I'm going home.'

'Just before you depart, take a look into the sergeants' room, would you?'

Shoving a much-needed Gauloise between his lips, Pel allowed Darcy to escort him down the corridor.

There appeared to be an auction taking place.

'*Vingt francs le kilo, c'est une affaire!*' Misset's voice was heard above the general din in the room.

'Mother of God!' Pel exploded. 'What's going on here? This isn't a sodding *épicerie*!'

'No, Patron,' Misset replied, 'but the wife stuffed the fifty kilos of tomatoes you bought at the market and she doesn't have room for them in the freezer. Go on.' He grinned stupidly. 'A kilo for twenty francs, it's a bargain.'

'Sell them to Darcy,' Pel growled, 'he's got a growing family.'

'So have I,' Nosjean added. 'Mijo's pregnant again.'

Pel folded his glasses and pushed them into a convenient pocket. 'Darcy,' he said wearily, 'get me out of this madhouse.'